NO TIME FOR FAST TIME

No Time for Fast Time
Copyright © 2022 by Harlan Wells

Front cover by the author, altered from design on canva.com.
Layout and edits by Jerri-Jo Idarius of https://creation-designs.com
Printed by KDPAmazon, a DBA of On-Demand Publishing, LLC,
part of the Amazon group of companies.

Harlan Wells: cardinalfire@gmail.com

ISBN: 9798831430202

Adult Fiction

No Time For Fast Time

By

Harlan Wells

Cardinal Fire Publishing

2022

No Time For Fast Time

"Government officials will meet at the nation's capital today to discuss further control measures to curtail the spread of the deadly RABID-30 outbreak. The rabies-like virus starts with flu-like symptoms such as a fever and headache and can rapidly advance to cause severe mental deterioration as well as lung and heart failure. Symptoms can include slight or partial paralysis, anxiety, insomnia, paranoia, hallucinations and extreme aggression. The virus spreads via physical contact, although mounting evidence suggests it can also be airborne. It has infected over 100 million people worldwide and has claimed the lives of nearly 2 million."

Arian Guyd rolled up the driver side window nearly all the way, quieting the whipping desert air. The report continued: "Three months into the global pandemic and, although countries such as China, South Korea and Russia are showing modest signs of containment, much of Western Europe and the US are struggling to flatten the curve. Hospitals, testing centers, and other medical facilities are overwhelmed. Medical personnel are working around the clock while medical supplies are rapidly depleting. The president will meet with representatives of the WHO today to discuss . . ." Arian reached over and cut the volume. He rolled his window back down and the whipping air howled past his ear.

Arian worked for FoodCORP delivery corporation. He was in his late twenties. He had an average build, had short black hair and deep soulful eyes that were at once unassuming and profound. He had a thick forehead that was often angled slightly upward, as if defiantly bucking back against the world.

He recalled the round hazel eyes of his fiancée, laden with fears and paranoias. Kirsten worked as a nurse: 'What ifs' surrounding the pandemic came pounding into her brain like a hammer as she washed her hands in the sink, three times over.

Honey, you are HOME Now; relax! he remembered telling her, while reaching over to shut off the faucet.

But there are lives at stake! she said. *What if I don't decontaminate thoroughly enough? If I miss even the slightest step, I put someone's life at risk. It can happen so fast.* She reached up for the faucet.

You washed your hands three times already, Arian recalled grabbing her wrist and watching as tears welled up in her eyes.

Dozens of newly infected patients are pouring into Intensive Care every hour of every day! She shook her head. *Decontaminating and taking temperatures . . . taking saliva samples . . . removing the sure-to-be dead to make room for those who might survive . . .* Kirsten machine-gunned out the words.

STOP! Arian recalled grabbing her shoulders and saying, *You have to disconnect at some point. You are home now. You spend twelve to fourteen hours a day saving lives. HOME is NOT the HOSPITAL.* She stared back; face pale white, eyes frozen in her skull. He pulled her close, wrapping his arms around her shaking body. *You are home, safe. There Are no sick people here, no virus. It's just the two of us, right here at home, safe and sound. Everything is going to be ok . . . everything is going to be OK.*

As the memory dispersed, he found himself back in his delivery truck—alone with the dry shrubs and punishing heat of the Mojave Desert. The air whipped up the smell of hot asphalt as he wiped sweat along his hairline with the back of his free hand. He wore disposable gloves, as per official safety measures during the pandemic. Sweat gathered between his fingers and around his engagement ring, but he refused to take it off. Though he was required to wear a medical-grade face mask, he only did so when around other people.

Arian wore a polo shirt with the moniker 'FoodCORP and Pharmacy' written across the chest. He wore khaki pants and high top boots. What wasn't part of the company dress code was a hammer, which he kept beneath the seat of the six-wheeled, eight-ton truck.

Now, more than ever, there were too many uncertainties, too many 'what ifs' in this No Man's Land.

Isn't the rise in temperature supposed to kill the damn virus? he thought, gazing past the vast spread of parched sand, rock, and cacti, out towards the horizon where the Sierra Nevadas stretched out as far as the eye could see, like an ominous gate to another world. The highway was a decayed, sun-blanched tributary through a hopeless parable at life's end. The longer it stretched on, and the more the miles were spat out, the more it felt like he was neither coming nor going, just suspended in limbo between wastelands. The engine hummed over the highway like a dying mantra encouraging life to hold on.

He passed ruins of old farming communities with long, unused driveways, leaning fences and rusted gates. He passed old abandoned barns with portions of their walls missing and dusty dried-up shingles along their roofs—sprung up in the distance like forgotten scarecrows. The occasional blown tire dotted the roadside along with the occasional burnt-out frame of a car. He noted a patch of Joshua trees a few hundred yards off the highway. A lifeless body hanging from one of the trees leapt out and caught his eye.

"Jesus!" Arian jerked the steering wheel and sent the truck swerving. He steadied the wheel and looked back through the side view mirror. The hanging body and patch of Joshua trees disappeared into a blip behind him.

"Must be the heat." He reached for a bottle of water in the center console.

As the workdays stretched on, it seemed no amount of podcasts, music, radio or other distractions could break the wasteland's monotonous spell. Yet he cultivated the habit of always staying connected to the digital world.

"Must be the heat," he repeated, wiping his brow and pushing the image of the hanging body from his mind. It would be a few more hours until he reached Relocation Camp A1.

Arian eased off the gas as a large sign came into view: It read, 'Check Point.' Police and highway patrol vehicles were parked along the road. Two large militarized police officers stood next to a police van. One of the officers waved Arian on, so he pulled off the highway and stopped in front of the two officers. One walked over to the driver's side of Arian's truck while the other, much larger officer, stepped over to the passenger side. He was holding an automatic weapon across his chest. Both men wore disposable medical gloves and masks. Arian rolled down his window.

"Name?" The officer said.

"Arian Guyd. FoodCORP and Pharmacy," Arian said, extending his driver's license. The officer looked it over. He lifted his palm signaling Arian to 'stand by.'

"FoodCORP?" The officer said finally.

"FoodCORP," Arian repeated with a nod.

The officer said something into the walkie-talkie. It murmured back with static and then the officer said "Step out of the vehicle."

Arian got out. The officer pressed a thermometer gun to Arian's forehead, his eyes narrowing at the sweat lining Arian's hairline. The officer had pale blue eyes and pupils that stabbed forward like a knife. Above his eyes hovered silver eyebrows combed into arched perfection. He pulled the thermometer away and waved on a third officer, who circled the truck wearing a full-body medical suit and a backpack filled with antiseptic. With a long-nozzle spray gun, he covered the truck in a thin cloud.

"Open her up," The officer circled around. Arian unlatched the side door of the truck and lifted it overhead. Totes filled with food, toiletries and pharmaceuticals were stocked in a series of vertical compartments.

The officer pulled out a tote and rummaged around with his free hand. He then sent a quick glance at Arian, who was sweating in the heat. The officer shoved the tote back into place and walked over to the driver side window and looked inside. He turned and sent one last glance at Arian, then nodded.

Arian shut the side door and climbed back into the driver seat.

"All clear for FoodCORP," the officer said, waving Arian on.

I come here almost every day, you'd think these jerks would at least try to remember my face, Arian thought, driving through the open gate, entering Relocation Camp A1.

On the drive back home to Los Angeles County that night, rolling across the endless spread of desert dubbed 'No Man's Land' by the popular news media, a body hanging from a Joshua tree again flashed by his periphery. Arian turned to look, but there was nothing. *No Man's Land,* he thought, holding the image of the hanging body in his mind's eye.

The heat of the day had begun to settle, and the desert temps were dropping. Soon a chill would come to the flatlands. The clock on the radio read 20:12.

Another twelve-hour day by the time it's all said and done.

Arian's mind sank to semi-dreariness as the highway slithered over the land like a serpent. The gentle sway of the truck, now empty, over the snaking highway was a subtle lull to dreamland. *Twelve hours, two Relocation Camps, nearly 600 miles….* His thoughts had a distant, foggy quality, like the last of the smog clouds outside of LA just before the initial run into the desert.

He was lucky to have the job. Food delivery was considered 'essential' during the pandemic. Most jobs were done from home. The nationwide stay-at-home/work-from-home order came last month, forcing the country indoors. You were only allowed out to buy groceries, medication or to the doctor. Everyone had to have a legitimate reason to be outdoors, or risk a fine or even imprisonment.

Arian was hired just two weeks before the pandemic hit the States, and only a few months before he proposed to Kirsten. He needed the money and, with the economy projected to hit rock bottom, he eagerly signed on. Kirsten worked in one of the main hospitals in L.A. They lived in San Bernardino, where life was cheaper.

That night, slipping into bed alongside his sleeping fiancée, his eyes wandered the simple white ceiling in the semi-darkness. He imagined Interstate 15 spreading like a stream through the rocky clumps of the ceiling plaster. He traced the route from Relocation Camp A1 just outside Barstow, to A2 near the Nevada border. There was talk of a third Camp springing up on the other side of the Angeles National Forest. And if so, FoodCORP would be adding more shifts to the workload. *More . . . work . . .* he thought, glancing over at Kirsten who was curled up in the fetal position, her back to him.

He wanted to lean over and kiss her cheek, to smell her hair, to feel the warmth of her skin. But he couldn't bring himself to wake her. Even though she was adamant about seeing him, even if it was just for a few minutes in the late hours of the night, he couldn't bring himself to jostle her from sleep. He knew the consequences, and it drove a stake of loneliness deep into his chest. Not waking her would mean another three days of twelve hour shifts and only seeing her for a few minutes, face-to-face each day at breakfast. He felt dirty, infected without the gloves and mask. Although showered and thoroughly cleaned, he felt he was contaminating the bed, that his very breath was a threat to life. And with her incessant fears of infection, the last thing he wanted was to be a part of the problem.

Don't be absurd, he thought, *I work out in the middle of the desert; I hardly come in contact with anyone. And Kirsten works at the hospital. They use PPE and have strict decontamination procedures. We're fine.* A news report detailing the percentage of nurses and medical staff confirmed positive with the virus, and the likelihood of infecting family at home, came to mind.

Bullshit! He thought. *We're in our late 20's. We'd survive the infection. We'd self-quarantine, keep others safe . . . but we'd miss work. And work is money.* He thumbed his engagement ring. He closed his eyes and took a deep breath. He exhaled, letting as little air pass from his nose as possible, as if he was slowly releasing a bioweapon. As his world faded into darkness, he felt a sudden sense of isolation and loneliness as he lay next to his fiancée—a feeling no different than his daily 600 mile-drive through the desert.

❧

Arian's daily routine was as monotonous as the barren land he crossed. He woke up at 8 am, drove to the FoodCORP warehouse in L.A., stocked the truck and hit the road by 10 am, made two deliveries, one at each of the Relocation Camps and then drove back to the warehouse to drop off the truck and finally head for home.

The highlight of his day was having breakfast with Kirsten, the solitary ten minutes they were able to share; to speak, interact . . . and touch. Text messages and calls became rarer. He didn't want to distract her at work, and she really didn't have any time as it was—aside from her lunch break which was often rushed or cut short in order to tend to the influx of patients. If they weren't careful, their collective stresses could spark unnecessary conflict. This day, as he drove across the desert, a memory came to him:

"Why didn't you wake me last night?" Kirsten had said, looking up from her coffee mug.

"Honey, you need proper rest."

"Rest?" She set the mug down with a thump and rubbed her eyes. "Rest? I don't even know what that is anymore," she said.

Arian moved his chair over and lay his palm over her thigh, "It's going to be ok. We'll get through this."

"Dear God, I hope so," she said.

"This Saturday, I'm free. We're stuck indoors whether we like it or not. We'll have a quiet, relaxing day together, here at home—just the two of us."

"It depends how bad it is at the hospital over the weekend. I might have to work" Kirsten said.

7

"I thought you were supposed to have at least one day off?"

"With the way things are going, I'm not sure I can," she said.

"I see."

"Dammit," she said.

"What?"

"I want to see you," Kirsten said. "This pandemic, it's . . . it's . . ." her voice dropped.

"I know honey. I know. We're all feeling it. The world is a crazy place right now, but we'll get through this, I promise," he said, rubbing her shoulder.

"I hope you're right," she said. She leaned forward and rested her shoulder under his chin. He threw his arms around her.

"I miss you," she said.

"I miss you too sweetheart." The smell of her hair, her cheek pressed to his chest, his arms against her back and shoulders, he could almost feel her skin, her flesh . . . human con-tact. The memory dispersed, and he was back on the road, driving.

They say the world will be changed forever. Things can't possibly return to the way they were. Has the pandemic—the infections and deaths, job losses, divorces and suicides already permanently changed the world? Then came the feeling that the world was indeed lost forever—it had stopped spinning, only to pick up speed and spin faster than anyone ever could have imagined.

What can we do? Kirsten is making a difference, his thoughts went on. *She's a nurse; she's saving lives. I'm delivering much-needed food and medicine. I have one of the only "essential" jobs. We are doing our part, we are making a difference . . . change. Yes, the world will change. Perhaps change is what we need?*

He thought about the reduced pollution as a result of the pandemic; the empty streets and highways, the grounded airlines, animals and marine life reclaiming their former habitants—taking back the people-free and trash-free streets, mountainsides and beaches. With bars, clubs, restaurants, movie theaters, and sporting events shut down, people were forced to entertain themselves at home, be with family.

People were spending more quality time with loved ones, catching up and reconnecting with old friends and relatives through video calls and social media.

People are dying and people's freedoms are being taken away, yet many are feeling grateful for the simple things, rediscovering what's truly important in their lives. Appreciation of everyday things we normally take for granted was becoming the 'new cool.'

People were exercising indoors with homemade gyms and online workout programs. People were cooking more, and eating healthier, homemade meals. But still others were over-eating and drinking to excess.

Take the good with the bad. His mind wandered. He thought of his parents; both were in their seventies and he thought about what it would be like to lose them. *I gotta call them.*

He thought about the Relocation Camps and how they received several food deliveries, depending on how many new people were infected and 'relocated' any given week. There were several food and grocery delivery companies running, as now a growing number of the population, not just the elderly, disabled or the retired, were having their food delivered due to restaurant closures and stay-at-home-orders. Delivery trucks seemed to be the only vehicles on the road. Deliveries by bike were common in the inner cities, but for the remote areas, Relocation Camps consolidated the infected and kept them away from densely populated, high-risk areas. These Camps were makeshift hospitals that took the overflow of patients from collapsed inner-city hospitals. They were set up outside of most major cities across the country.–The virus had up to a fourteen-day incubation period and could live for several days on metallic, plastic, and wooden surfaces.

His thoughts lifted, clearing like a light, wafting mist. Back in the present, in the truck, eyes on the lulling highway, Arian's workday was coming to an end. He wiped his brow, and checked his temperature with the back of his hand. He eyed a thermometer gun in the center console of the truck. All drivers were required to check their temperature at the beginning and end of every shift, and immediately report any sign of a fever or flu-like symptoms.

I thought the heat was supposed to kill the damn virus. He repeated his daily monologue. *Another day in the books, another 12 hours on the road before it's all said and done.* The clock on the dashboard read "20:04." The open road yawned as the sun began its descent over the horizon, squeezing out a strip of light that shone purple in the dark recesses of the mountains. His eyes grew heavy as the tires rolling over the highway lulled him ever so subtly into the cradle.

He felt a ping in his bladder and eased off the gas. He pulled onto the shoulder of the road, flipped on the hazard lights and got out of the truck. He walked around to the back of the truck, unzipped his fly and wetted the ground next to the tire. The cooling desert air and the relief in his bladder soothed him. He took a long look up the highway ahead. It appeared as the tail of a lizard zig-zagging across space and time. He zipped up his fly and started back to the driver's side of the truck. Suddenly, a loud click came from behind.

"Put yer hands up" came a hoarse voice from the darkness. Arian froze and raised his hands.

"Turn around," the voice commanded.

Arian turned, staring down the barrel of a shotgun held by a large, middle-aged man wearing a medical mask that covered the bottom half of his face. He was dressed in a long-sleeve flannel shirt and old, worn overalls. He was obese; had a large gut, flabby arms and neck. Behind him was a rusty white pickup truck with its lights off, idling in the coming night. Arian didn't get a good look at the driver, but noted a dark, powerful presence behind the wheel. The man pulled his eyes from the shotgun and looked squarely at Arian. His eyes shimmered in the twilight, like light reflecting off water. However, the look in his eyes and the condition of his pitted ruddy skin made the man appear strangely ill, like a diseased pig.

A pig, yes, that's it. He's a damn pig, Arian thought. The Pig raised the barrel back to his eye, as if he'd heard Arian's thoughts.

"I don't have much cash, but take everything . . ." Arian said, trembling.

"Shut up!" The Pig squealed. Just then, the rusty pickup emerged from the semi-darkness like a mechanical lizard. It pulled forward and stopped alongside the piggish man. The driver stared at Arian through the window; a slender pale face. It was maskless and had close-set eyes that looked down the end of a long sharp nose. His mouth hung dumbly, opened in a slack-jaw with a forked tongue that lay drooping over his bottom lip. His lips were wet with drool and spittle. He wore a straw hat over tufts of what looked to be red hair, jutting out in all directions.

"You infected?" The Pig asked, aiming the shotgun between Arian's eyes.

"No," Arian said.

The Pig looked Arian up and down.

"We're tested constantly . . . we disinfect the truck every day . . . we wear gloves and masks."

The Pig held an incredulous gaze.

"I have a thermometer in the truck," Arian added.

The Pig squinted, still aiming the shotgun between Arian's eyes. The Pig said finally: "Alright, now listen up."

❧

"Where are we going?" Arian broke the silence, hands on the wheel, eyes on the road ahead.

"Shut up n' drive" the Pig said from the passenger seat. He was leaning against the window and pressing the barrel of the shotgun into Arian's crotch. Arian's thoughts darted back and forth between fight or flight.

The hammer beneath the seat! You fool, what's a hammer going to do against a shotgun? he thought, as a vision of the shotgun blasting his face off as he reached down for the hammer flashed through his mind. Any sudden movement risked crashing the truck, or getting his jewels blown to bits . . . or both.

What if I can wrestle the gun away from him? Who am I kidding? I don't even know how to shoot. Something deep in the back of the Pig's eyes told him nothing would come easy. There was also the other guy following closely behind them in the pickup.

Is he armed? Sweat fell from Arian's brow and slid down into his eyes. He felt the urge to wipe it. *Can't give the Pig reason to shoot.* Arian's ring finger twitched. The sweat stung his eyes.

"Don't you try nuthin' funny now" the Pig said.

"Of course not," Arian managed.

He musta seen me flinch, Arian thought, carefully posturing up, trying not to appear threatening. *The Pig's accent sounds forced. It's southern for sure, old country. But forced, exaggerated. Or maybe that delayed, labored drawl of his is a sign of his failing health? His skin is terrible and he's grotesquely overweight.* Although they were both wearing masks, the Pig's heavy breathing further added to Arian's RABID-30 paranoia.

"Ya see that ol' road there, comin' up on the right?" The Pig signaled with a nod.

"Yes," Arian said.

"Take it," said the Pig.

Arian eased onto the shoulder and took the old farm road. He glanced into the side view mirror and saw the white pickup following close behind.

"Don't ya mind him, keep yer eyes on the road" the Pig said.

They drove on for some time, the old gravelly road pulling further away from the highway. The road gradually disintegrated into raw desert, becoming a tract of flat, unforgiving indifference. Finally, they reached a patch of cacti and a large scattering of rocks.

"Turn here," the Pig said. Arian did so, his hand trembling at the wheel, holding an image of his beautiful fiancée in his mind's eye.

Please don't kill me, please don't kill me, he prayed. The Pig's gaze was steady over him and again he felt as if the Pig could read his thoughts.

"Stop," the Pig said. Arian hit the brakes, dispersing the image of Kirsten into the unfiltered dark. He found himself in an obscure rocky outcropping a ways off the highway.

"Shut 'er off," the Pig said.

Arian killed the engine and they sat unmoving in the darkness. A moment later, the white pickup crawled up alongside them. The driver got out and walked up.

"Get out" the Pig nudged Arian with the barrel of the shotgun. "An' keep them hands up."

Arian got out and raised his hands: "Ok, ok. Don't shoot."

The Pig slid out, and the other driver walked around, nudging Arian towards the FoodCORP truck's storage compartment.

"Open 'er up" the Pig said, joining them.

Arian unlocked the door and raised it overhead. The driver of the pickup started taking the totes of groceries from Arian's truck and loading them into the back of the pickup. He was at least a head taller than Arian, and his hands were twice as big as his. His palms were large and flat, and he had long scaly fingers with sharp nails. He too wore a plaid shirt, a belt with a large buckle, and dirty, beat up jeans that sagged from his waist.

Mid 20's? His feet moved effortlessly over the desert in a slither, like a snake or lizard. His movements were smooth and efficient with no wasted effort. His slithery movement, his hands, eyes and tongue were reptilian, somehow. But he was wiry, with a strong frame. It belied his goofy, moronic face and hanging slack jaw. He lifted the totes with ease, even the totes filled with five-liter bottles of water didn't phase him.

"C'mon!" The Pig said, waving the barrel. Arian jumped in, helping transfer the groceries to the pickup.

They finished loading and got inside the pickup of the tall thin man with a forked tongue and reptilian-like skin. The man drove back towards the highway. Arian sat beside him in the passenger seat. The Pig was sitting in the back of the pickup, nestled among the mountain of stolen groceries, with the barrel of the shotgun shoved through the opened window at the back of the cab, the barrel mere inches from Arian's head. The cab was dusty and smelled like tobacco and gasoline. The dashboard had an empty pouch of roll-your-own tobacco plopped lazily over it; above it was a dusty windshield with a small crack in the corner. The radio was off and was choked with dust in all of its small corners and crevices. Arian's seat was torn along the seams, and its padding bled out like a squashed sandwich.

The man's physicality was even more evident in close quarters. And his strange, reptilian energy suffocated the air like an invisible vapor . . a shadow, forever at his side. This shadowy energy was sensed but not seen. Or was it a trick of the senses? A play of fears in the night?

Arian watched as his truck burned into the night from the side view mirror, shrinking away ever so slowly as they pulled away. The fingers of the flames leapt up to the sky, in them, the truck's final pleas silenced by the desert night. As bright as the fire burned, and as eagerly as the truck cried out in its dying breath, Arian knew it wouldn't be seen. And neither would he. *Why have I been taken hostage rather than shot, left for dead or burned up along with the truck? Were they trying to make it look like another desert suicide? Instead I've been taken . . . but to where?*

His heart pounded in his chest as a vision flashed by of him opening the door and making a run for it. But those long arms, giant hands and the belying, capable movement of the Reptilian driver made him second guess it. Besides, something told him that the Pig was a good shot and, at point-blank range, an escape attempt would mean instant death. And even if he did escape, he couldn't go anywhere or call anyone. His cellphone was in the center console of his delivery truck, burned up along with the rest of it. If he did escape, he'd be alone . . . lost in the middle of a desert wasteland. Who knows when the next vehicle would pass? Aside from the occasional highway patrol or other such grocery or freight truck, he was one of the only people on the road, ever.

His thoughts raced. He dared not move a muscle. When he thought of escape, his heart kicked up and sweat drained out his pores. He once again felt the intensity of those damn pig-like eyes burning over him. They burned like the tongues of flame roaring over his truck's sad frame. So brilliantly the fire raged, so incessant were Arian's scattered, panicked thoughts . . . not to be seen or heard except by the silent contract between night and sand. Unseen and unheard, except by those damn, pig-like eyes . . .

Shut up, Arian told himself, biting down on his lower lip. An eternity could have passed or mere seconds, and he wouldn't have known the difference. To him, time had stopped. Everything he knew before ceased to exist.

The driver reached under his seat. Arian stiffened.

"Relax," the Pig ordered, sticking the barrel closer to Arian's head. The driver produced a black bandana and extended it to Arian between his scaly, lizard-like fingers.

"Put it over yer eyes" the Pig said. Arian hesitated as the driver's hand loomed closer.

"C'mon" the Pig grunted. Arian wrapped the bandana around his eyes and tied it.

It's so damn dark out, I can't see anything anyway, Arian thought. The blindfold and darkness did little to calm his nerves as images rushed in of Kirsten. Her face contorted with concern—not for the virus, not about her obsessive washing of her hands, not about those certain to die being removed from hospital beds to make room for those that might have a chance to survive, but concern for her missing husband-to-be. In his mind's eye, he watched her pace the kitchen floor, slam her fist down on the counter, then spill over, burying her face in her hands. He forced his mind back to the present. He went to wipe his tear-welled eyes, but stopped suddenly, *a sign of weakness, the Pig is watching.*

The pickup made a 180 degree turn. They drove on for some time in the direction from which they had come.

Did the driver just get lost, or are they trying to confuse me? How would I know where the hell we are, let alone where we are GOING? I'm blindfolded, and it's pitch black out there. Even if I could see, the desert all looks the same. What on earth could they be hiding? The pickup pulled off the road. The front wheels dipped, the chassis rocked, and the tires crawled over the desert floor. The Pig's breathing grew louder and he made a subtle movement in the silence. The driver shifted in his seat, and Arian could feel his dark energy shift too.

Did the Pig tap the driver's shoulder? Did he whisper something or give him some kind of signal? Arian sat still.

If they were going to kill me, they would have done it already . . . no, they're not going to kill me . . . yet? They drove on for some time. The darkness forced Arian inward. He closed his eyes and thumbed at his engagement ring as if it were a rosary bead. Finally, the pickup came to a stop. The engine sputtered then died away.

"Don't move" the Pig nudged the barrel of the shotgun against the back of Arian's head. The driver got out, opened Arian's door and pulled him out. The driver's enormous hand and long thin fingers engulfed Arian's arm like a baseball mitt.

Holy crap, he could easily crush me with his bare hands, Arian thought.

He heard the Pig get down from the back of the pickup. His hefty, cumbersome footfalls neared.

"Hold still," the driver said. A blast of antiseptic sprayed against Arian's face. Arian turned his head away.

"Hold still dammit!" The spraying continued until covering him head-to-toe.

"Jesus!" Arian said, shivering.

"Alright," the driver said once the spraying stopped. The driver led him on, and then came the sound of whining hinges as he was led up a step and through a door. They went inside and his steps fell over creaky hardwood, as the driver slithered silently over the floor. They passed through what seemed to be a large living room. The Pig's bulky footfalls followed close behind.

The room was silent and suspicious, as if it was brewing a plot to rob a bank. It was dry, dusty, cold and uninviting. They crossed what seemed to be a hall, his footfalls echoing off the narrow walls. Arian could hear the Pig's footfalls following behind, but more so could feel the Pig watching. At the end of the hall, they passed through a door to what seemed to be a small room.

The driver hit a switch with his free hand, producing a faint yellow glow from above. The driver seemed to crouch down and lift something with his free hand. A long, creeping whine crept up from the floor. *A hatch?*

"There's a ladder," the driver said, nudging Arian down. Arian's feet searched for the ladder. The driver released his grip, and Arian got down on all fours and was able to find the top of the ladder with his foot.

"Go on," the driver said with an adolescent tone. It wasn't that it was high-pitched, but it was immature, simple. Arian descended the ladder using his hands and feet as feelers in the dark. He took a cautious step and kicked a pebble with the toe of his boot. The driver's slithering footfalls followed, descending the ladder. Arian ran his gloved fingers over a concrete wall. He stood up on his toes and touched the wood ceiling with the tip of his pointer finger. He sensed the driver approaching, his feet slithering across the ground nearly-inaudibly. He grabbed Arian by the arm, and pressed him back against the wall.

"On yer knees" he said. Arian kneeled, the concrete hard against his knees. He imagined the driver's forked tongue darting out as he talked. The dark cellar added to the intensity of the man's vapor-like energy, a romance born in nightmare. He raised Arian's arm and tied his wrist against a hanging cable, or chain.

Meathook? He then did the same with the other arm, so that Arian hung as if crucified, but with his knees on the concrete floor.

The driver stripped the medical mask off Arian's face and stretched duct tape in its place.

Hell, Arian thought, as the driver slithered back to the ladder and ascended in near-silence. He closed the hatch behind him, shutting out his dark reptilian energy along with the hatch's faint, ghostly light.

Arian awoke, finding himself down on his knees, wrists chained from above. His shoulders and arms were numb, useless to pull himself up. He stood slowly, legs wobbly beneath him. He stretched his arms, pulling his shoulders back and thrusting his chest forward. Pain shot down his spine and hip. Blood rushed to his extremities; tingling up to his head.

He tried to lower the blindfold from his eyes with the rotation of his shoulder, but couldn't quite reach. Unable to see anything beyond the darkness of the blindfold, he swung his leg forward and poked around with the toe of his boot.

He poked around for the ladder, but couldn't reach it. He kicked at the concrete wall behind him, and with the heel of his boot, surveyed every available inch of the wall.

He reached up, grabbed the chains and was able to lift his feet off the floor. He hung for a moment, then bounced and swung forward, tugging and pulling hard against the chains. *These chains aren't going anywhere.*

Kirsten! He jerked against the chains, screaming. He jerked again, harder this time. He screamed again, and kicked the wall behind him. He tugged and pulled at the chains with all his might, screaming into the strip of duct tape across his mouth. His muffled cries went unanswered in the silence. He fell to his knees, catching his breath.

Take it easy, he thought, addressing his beating heart. The basement was completely still, silent and dark, the Unmovabe Mover indifferent to his plight. And so he knelt, blind in the silence, listening intently. No sound of footsteps, no opening or closing of doors, nothing but an old house at rest. Now he too was unmoving, except his restless mind, ping-ponging between fears; conjuring images of . . . what he feared to lose. And there came too, the urge, the subconscious need to check his cell phone for a text, an email—for any tidbit of information, photo, MEME, GIF, anything to break the monotony. He usually kept his phone in his front right pocket, but it was gone and there was the feeling that part of him was lost forever.

Standing tired his legs, but it rested his arms and shoulders, which grew stiff with pain as blood drained from them. So he would alternate between standing, squatting with his knees bent while flatfooted, to kneeling on both knees with his arms hanging from the chains—the position the Reptilian driver had forced him into when he first arrived. It was in these positions that he learned to sleep. It was a kind of half-sleep, with one eye open. He felt, in a strange way at least, that he was able to escape. In compartmentalizing the body, mind and spirit—one part escaped the suffering while the other embraced it.

It could have been a matter of hours or days, but it felt like weeks until the hatch opened again. He was awakened from a catatonic-like state, his eyes suddenly opened, frozen and fixed behind the blindfold, his mind lost in the image of himself swimming to a far-off utopia, when he heard a nearly soundless slither approach the hatch. The slithering was so subtle, he doubted he normally would have heard it, except that he had become hyper-aware, his hearing hyper-acute. The basement rarely came to life and, when it did, it was with the sound of footfalls along the floorboards above. They usually came from somewhere down the hallway, or from the room he had first been led through. There was the occasional sound of the flow of water that ran through piping overhead and drained down along the opposite wall. The hatch opened slowly, groaning. Then came the slither of the reptilian driver, descending the ladder.

That's what he is, he's a damn reptile, Arian thought. *The fatso is a pig, and the tall, slithering slack-jaw is a reptile. That's it. These bastards aren't human.*

As the "Reptile" neared, Arian felt the dark energy that followed him intensify. Suddenly, a thin spray of liquid blasted Arian's face.

"Ugh," Arian moaned into the duct tape. Another two blasts covered Arian's hands.

Antiseptic, Arian thought as the smell choked the air. The Reptile reached his thin lizard fingers over and stripped off the duct tape.

"You bastards!" Arian said, his pulse kicked up, his heart pumping blood, drawing more energy than he could really muster.

"What are you—?"

"Shut up" the Reptile said, in a dopey, boyish voice. The Reptile set something on the concrete floor, clinking against the concrete. He reached over and undid Arian's right wrist. Arian lifted the blindfold up past his eyes. The Reptile stood just out of reach, his head stooping beneath the ceiling.

My God he's tall, Arian thought, reeling back.

"Eat!" The Reptile pointed to a plate at his feet. Arian reached for the plate, his face at the Reptile's feet.

"You want me to kiss your feet while I'm down here?" Arian said. He picked up a piece of stale bread from the plate. *Bread?* he thought, shoving it in his mouth. Beside the plate, just out of reach, was a bowl of water.

"Is that a dog bowl?" Arian said.

"Eat!" the Reptile insisted.

Arian chewed on, licking his lips as bread crumbs fell down his chin. He lost himself in a compulsive, primitive gorging, a long-lost salivary treat, and when he finally came too, it was like a storm had passed, and he found himself at the mercy of a demon. He straightened up and let out a belch.

"Water . . . " Arian said. The Reptile stared back with a detached glare.

"Please," Arian pleaded. The Reptile reached down with his long arm, like a Titan showing pity on a mortal, picked up the bowl and extended it. Arian reached for it, but as he did so, the Reptile pulled it back, just out of Arian's reach, then thrust the bowl forward, splashing Arian's face.

"What the hell's the matter with you?" Arian wiped his face. The Reptile stared dumbly back. The Reptile's hair appeared pumpkin orange beneath the soft light slanting down from the hatch. His eyes were locked in their usual close-set and near cross-eye, his mouth open, jaw-hanging with drool spilling down his lower lip. The Reptile eyed Arian's tongue as it lapped water up from the corners of his mouth, and just then, the Reptile's own, forked tongue darted out of his mouth. "What the—?" Arian reeled back. The Reptile's hanging jaw did its best to pull his face into a semi-smile. He extended the half-full bowl of water. Arian looked back at him, defenses drawn.

"Drink" the Reptile said, back to that dopey, slack jawed-expression of his.

Arian took the bowl and emptied it with a large gulp. The Reptile took the bowl, set it aside and said; "Wipe yer mouth." Arian did so. The Reptile pulled out a roll of duct tape and stretched a piece over Arian's mouth. Arian caught a final glance of the Reptile's semi-smile before he put the blindfold back over his eyes, casting him back into the dark world. In the near-silence, Arian heard him slither back towards the ladder. He then heard the hatch creak open, and then a dull but punctuating thud as it closed, like a half-hearted judge's gavel.

❧

"I understand Ma'am. I really do. As I said, we reported the vehicle missing, filed the Missing-Persons Report and have officers on the case," police Chief Eric Dalton said into the phone.

"It's been six days!" Kirsten said. "Somebody must have reported something!"

"We're doing what we can."

"And what exactly is it that you're doing?"

"Ma'am, look. We're working around the clock. Not only are we dealing with a global pandemic, the likes of which the world has never seen, but divorce rates are skyrocketing, and domestic violence is up. Husbands are disappearing on their wives, leaving their families. Depression and suici . . . " the officer's words fell off.

"I know . . . I know," Kirsten said.

Police Chief Dalton went on: "People are losing their loved ones to the damn virus, this damn pandemic . . . not to mention millions of dollars in loss of income . . . businesses are declaring bankruptcy left and right. People are panic-buying rice, pasta, toothpaste. There are nationwide break-ins at warehouses and port yards. . . . They're killing each other over toilet paper, for Christ's sake!"

"I know you have your hands full, but Arian isn't the type to do any of these things. He wouldn't just walk out on me . . . or give up," Kirsten said.

"We are doing what we can," Dalton said.

"Arian . . ." She wiped away a tear. "He could have gotten into an accident on the road—the long drive, the twelve-to-fourteen hour shifts. . . ."

"Ma'am, as I said, there were no traffic accidents reported for April 13th. Highway patrol has their eyes and ears on the Mojave. If he was involved in an accident, we would have found out about it by now."

"Did you track his phone?"

"We have AT&T looking into it."

"You can send out more patrols, trace his work route—I provided all the FoodCORP route information to you. . . ."

"Ma'am, we have officers and highway patrol on the job. We are doing everything we can." The line fell silent, aside from the sound of Kirsten's heavy breathing. "We appreciate your patience," Dalton said, then hung up.

Kirsten exhaled a long, aspirated "Jesus," and dropped the phone from her ear. She stood suspended in time, floating in the anxiety of non-movement. An image of Arian's smiling face hung in her mind—days after their engagement—his eyes filled with joy and the promise of their future together.

She dared not look at pictures of him too often. The pictures on her phone or in photo albums around the house could quickly throw her off-balance. It was bad enough when she looked at his framed graduation portrait, or even worse, the picture of their Puerto Vallarta trip on the mantle; two sand-combing love birds in full honeymoon-phase-bloom, youth and innocence bursting forth unadulterated, showing in the nucleus of four eyes locked in as one, reflecting the same dreams, the same fearlessness to be a part of a better world . . . together. His eyes . . . and his smile of all smiles. It was a smile that wanted nothing more than to swallow the world with its kindness. It only made it worse. She contemplated taking the pictures down, shutting away the beautiful, painful remembrance. But keeping his smiling face visible to the world is what gave her hope; it's what kept him alive.

Despite the economic downturn, despite the changing world, the food shortages, suicides, the geo-political fear-mongering, and rampant conspiracy theories, Arian always smiled on. She was a strong, resilient woman, and he was loyal to a fault—fair and hopeful. Tirelessly hopeful. His positivity kept the gears turning, the engine steaming. She was the motor, but he was the 'why'. That's what made them the 'super couple,' their friends said. They fed off each other, brought each other up. They were equals. Together they ran a self-perpetuating machine of human power, human potential. Planting seed, sewing both individually and collectively, a super couple of the future, a model for generations to come. Things didn't have to be forced, they just needed time to coalesce and be given room to grow.

Now the machine ran at half-speed, chugging and sputtering on. Oil and grease and smoke belched and spewed out from its cogs and seals. The machine plodded along a burdened path, gears wearing, grinding down, beat and tired. She shrugged her head, dispersing the image of his smile and the beautiful organic machine that they were—dispersing it into a million vicious, infinitesimally small fragments.

She stood in the kitchen, head hanging over the countertop, her reflection looking back at her from in the glossy laminate. Suddenly, she reached for her phone.

"Angela—"

"Hey Kirsten, what's up? Any news?"

"No, not yet."

"Hang in there. Our thoughts and prayers are with you and Arian."

"Thanks. It means a lot," Kirsten said.

"Of course. Let me know if you need anything."

"Well, actually. I have an idea."

"Yeah, what is it?" Angela asked.

"Well, do you remember the name of that P.I. you hired years ago?"

"The P.I.?"

"Yeah, the private investigator."

"Private investigator?"

"The one you hired to catch Eric . . . cheating."

"Oh God!"

"I can't believe you."

"Sorry to bring it up, but—"

"For Christ's sake . . ."

"Look I'm sorry, but I need the P.I.'s contact."

"Yeah, ok. But that was some years ago now. I don't know if I still have it."

"Could you look please?"

"Hold on," Angela said.

"Alright."

"You're in luck, I have it. I'll send it to ya" Angela said after a minute.

"Thanks Ang, I really appreciate it."

"Yeah . . . no problem."

"And sorry."

"Ah, no worries, Eric is old news. It's over now. And really, this P.I. is the best. He could find Waldo in a haystack with a needle between his teeth," Anglela said.

"Perfect".

"Yeah, he's great. Good luck. Lemme know how it goes."

"Will do. Thanks Ang, you're the best . . . oh, and what's his name?"

"What?"

"The private investigator, what's his name?"

"Oh, his name is Hawk."

⁓

Arian's world grew into an increasingly torturous, unsolvable jigsaw. Discovering the motive for his capture became a nagging obsession. What he could remember of what little he'd seen of the basement came to him as faint and blurry flashes, strewn across a capricious mindscape. When his blindfold was removed and the Reptile fed him, he noted the spare concrete walls, the wooden ladder bathed in a faint orange light from the hatch above, and aged but sturdy wooden beams overhead.

The dry, dusty smell of the basement colored his thoughts, and the arid, stale air breathed over his skin, staining his flesh and charring his soul, coughing up ash, painting forgotten shadows. The images, smells and sensations played as disparate, fleeting parts. They haunted, and played with his sanity. But it wasn't just the visuals or smells or the thick dusty air; in its quietest moments, he could hear the basement tell its story. It leapt out and put a stranglehold on its audience. A tale of tribulation; a harrowing account of the violation of the human spirit.

Was Arian's experience simply just another chapter in an ongoing series of deaths? The casket was open, and it choked the air with its foul breath. The darkness burst forward, a violent explosion from some singular, finite point, desecrating the walls with its dead sperm, re-birthing the suffering so the world would know it; etching its howling call in one final, desperate plea.

He wanted to understand what was going on in a concrete way, what motive they could possibly have for his capture, but he also had the need to escape into meditation, fantasy and non-thought. But in time, he felt his mind grow stronger. He had no choice but to fortify it, callous it and build it up, piece by piece. Without the use of his cellphone, he had to entertain himself the old school way: with his mind. He would dredge the depths of his imagination to beat back the insanity.

He created imaginary villages and built up cities, kingdoms and empires like in the Age of Empires. He escaped into the world of Mario Kart. Vivid scenes from series like Game of Thrones and Vikings replayed in his mind. When he focused hard enough, he could even hear the sound of iron and steel clashing against chain mail, blood curdling screams and dying battle cries. He placed countries, capitals and flags across imaginary world maps. He did timetables. He repeated positive affirmations and mantras; "Everything's going to be ok, everything's going to be ok," and most of all, he visualized his freedom. He saw himself as a bird bursting through the bars of a steel cage and taking flight. He imagined cool air passing over his face and wings, floating with the clouds, light as a feather, untouched by darkness.

Yet, he grew increasingly lonely and began to imagine conversations with his parents and old friends from high school. He began to hold imaginary conversations with his old conspiracy theorist buddy, Auggie. Auggie dug deep into everything. Arian and their mutual college buddies used to tease Auggie for his elaborations. He hosted his own online forum, 'Auggie Digs Deeper.' That's why they called him Auggie, like an Auger that bores holes in the ground. He was the self-proclaimed 'underground king' of alternative media, conspiracy theories and the like.

He held the conviction that the JFK assassination was a CIA operation and cover-up, 9/11 was an inside job, and the 1947 Roswell Incident was a real event involving a UFO crash and E.T.'s. It wasn't that he wasn't possibly onto something, it was that his obsession with all things conspiratorial often took him to far out places. And those around him were often taken along for the ride—dragged into the undertow and unable to come up for air. Now, at this moment, his analytical ability would be appreciated. Arian imagined Auggie speaking to him, elbowing his way into his head and demystifying the murky darkness, like opening a decades-long closed curtain:

So what's their motive, what's their endgame? Auggie said. *Think about it, they stole everything from your truck because they need food, medicine, and medical supplies. They're older, less physically able. Well, at least the Pig is. The Reptile is younger than the Pig, more able-bodied. Perhaps the Reptile does all the work? They live in a remote wasteland; there are food shortages, a pandemic. They must have watched your truck drive by several times before they made their move. This was obviously premeditated. Remember the look in the Pig's eyes? This was not his first rodeo. Maybe other food trucks were hit too, maybe . . .*

Arian imagined Auggie's puffy, Einstein-like hair, jutting out in all directions, seemingly trying to connect to a collective consciousness, an extant thought-matrix. Auggie had unshaved whiskers on his cheeks and chin that he liked to stroke when thinking deeply. He had small dark eyes loaded with munitions that sat behind thin-rimmed, old-fashioned reading glasses.

Good 'ol Auggie, always there with a conspiracy theory when ya need him, Arian thought. But it was Kirsten that Arian thought of most.

He shut his eyes and repeated her name in a mantra, imagining a pure, thin white cloud of energy. The energy cloud was pumped full of pure serene energy and sent floating off to her. Off to deliver a message; *I'm ok; everything is going to be ok.* An energetic gift, a spirit telegraph, unseen but, if he focused hard enough, he could convince himself that she could feel it.

Kirsten . . . his mind jumped from topic to topic. It was like his brain had a built-in defense mechanism not allowing him to think too positively at the price of false hopes, nor would it allow him to think too negatively and spiral into insanity. He could not over- nor under-think, finding himself 'comfortably numb.' Pink Floyd's 'Wall' couldn't have been a more fitting narrative.

Four walls, he thought. *Four, three . . . ,* he counted down; *two . . . one. Once a day. The Reptile feeds me once a day. Never twice. Most days not at all. I have been fed three times . . . or has it been twice? Aside from the first week when I wasn't fed at all . . . just occasional water, just enough to keep death at bay . . . just enough to not waste away down here in this brimstone pit . . . The pit of the dead, the pit of snuffed flames and crushed souls. I have been here for nine, ten days? This would be day ten? Right? Shit. I have no idea.* Time was a language he didn't speak anymore. Only the faint overhead light coming and going with the opening of the hatch kept time. But it was of no time, of no schedule or of no basis. But it came and it went, irregularly regular.

Coming and going like the water, occasional bread and much less commonly, an egg or milk. Milk . . . fresh milk. FRESH COW'S MILK, Arian thought, his appetite whetting.

Auggie elbowed in: *What do you mean, 'cow's milk'?*

You know, cow's milk.

You mean milk from a cow?

Yes.

But fresh milk. You said 'fresh milk.'

Freshly milked cow's milk, yes.

They gave you fresh cow's milk?

Yes, once.

Like it was milked fresh that day?

Maybe.

So maybe you're on a ranch?

I don't know.

Don't they dress like cattle farmers?

Kind of.

You think maybe you're on an old cattle ranch, out in the middle of nowhere?

Yeah, could be.

C'mon, ya dope! Auggie rubbed it in, the way he always liked to triumph in his 'I was right's' and 'I told you so's'.

Ah who the hell knows. All I know is I'm chained here in some damn Godforsaken basement in the middle of the frickin' Mojave. Arian slumped down, pulling against the chains. He didn't have the energy to think anymore. His face was thinned, his body drained. He felt like his skull was breaking out of his face, pushing back against his skin. His bones sucking every ounce of liquid his flesh had to offer, stretching skin over ever-protruding bone. He did as much exercise as possible, pulling himself up on the chains, lifting himself with the strength of his weakened arms, doing a restricted version of pull-ups. It was agonizing, but it toughened him. He jogged in place to get his heart-rate up and he did calf-raises. Anything just to build what little muscle he could and not waste away into a forgotten skeleton.

But why keep me at the edge of life? Feed me just enough to keep me alive, vastly restrict my water intake—why psychologically torture me with this darkness, walk my mind steadily to the precipice of madness? Just to die a slow, painful death and waste away like the desert?

They are sick, you can't reason with madness. All-knowing Auggie spoke down from his ivory tower.

Well, whatever the hell they are. It isn't human.

It was never comfortable with the blindfold and the duct tape on his face, but as much as it suffocated him, it hardened him. His only opportunity to be cleaned was the damn splash of water from the water bowl. The 'shower'—the cleansing, the sense of renewal, the baptism—when the Reptile played his trick. Just to mind-fuck him. The 'shower' could come or it could not come at all that day, just like his 'meals.' But it would always come, eventually. Just to ensure Arian was controlled, a puppet, a play-thing. Just to remind him who the master is.

He thought of the Reptile's dopey, slack-jawed expression and how it beguiled his sickness and the cunning that he possessed. Sometimes Arian thought he could sense the Reptile's reptilian brain active in the shadows, active in his dark vapory energy where evil torments of the psyche are born.

"They are not human," Arian thought aloud. "Just get it over with and kill me, you fucks. Fear. Rule by fear. Isn't that a Machiavellian concept?" But it wasn't the fear of being splashed with water, it was the sudden splash of cold liquid over his body, the jolt, the shock, the not knowing if or when it would come. It was frighteningly refreshing. Arian grew to both hate and love it. Stockholm Syndrome? But the worst part, the most symbolic of the Reptile's acts of moral depravity was not splashing him with the very same water Arian needed to sustain his pitiful existence, no. This was not the worst of it. The worst part was the way he watched Arian's mouth after he had been splashed, his forked tongue darting out at the sight of Arian's.

That will haunt me forever, Arian thought. *Unless I cut out his goddamn tongue and hang it above my bed like a dreamcatcher. Yeah, that's it. As I lie in bed, off to sleep for the night, I'll look up at his severed tongue and it will rid me of all nightmares forever.* Arian lifted his head and screamed against the duct tape: "You bastards aren't human!" He pulled hard against the chains. He stomped on the concrete, he kicked the wall behind him. He fell to his knees, his fat stores digging deep for fuel. His lips begged for water. He was a forgotten non-hero, an unread script. His eyelids grew heavy and his world drew into an even greater darkness. Wrapped in a cold futility, he escaped, severing his mind and from his body.

"I'm not retired, per se, no," the man known as Hawk said.

"Perfect. I've got a case for you" Kirsten said.

"Well, I haven't worked in years."

"You remember working on a case for Angela Ramirez?"

"Ramirez?"

"Yes, Ramirez. She's a friend of mine."

"Doesn't ring a bell, I'm afraid."

"You caught her husband at the time, cheating."

"Ah, yes of course, Ramirez. I remember now. But that must have been . . . six or seven years ago."

"Did you move onto other things, or—?" Kirsten asked.

"Well, people don't seem to have the disposable income for private investigators these days."

"Don't worry, you'll be taken care of."

"It's not about the money, Ms. Kayble," Hawk said.

"Call me Kirsten."

"My last client was a wealthy trust-funder up in Beverly Hills. Was a missing person's case."

"What happened?"

"Well, the trust-funder's wife just disappeared one day. Turns out she was seeing another man. Started living with him. Someone who "really" loved her and someone she loved back, apparently. I guess the marriage was only about the money."

"Classic Hollywood story," Kirsten said.

"Yeah, I guess so . . . Kirsten, look," Hawk cleared his throat. "I'm old school. I'm not keen to stock anyone's social media, tap phone lines or any of that stuff. I find people. I hunt 'em down."

"That's precisely what I'm looking for," Kirsten said.

"And since my leg injury, I just don't get around like I used to."

"Listen, Hawk, it would mean the world to me, really."

"Um hmm" he hummed pensively. There was a brief silence.

"This is your fiancé, you said?"

"Yes," she said.

"He's been missing for a week or so, you say?"

"Yes," she choked up. There was another silence.

"They say you are the best," Kirsten said.

"Well," Hawk said dismissively, as if the 'best' were an abstract concept. He mulled over in the silence. He said finally; "Who the hell is allowed out of their homes these days anyway? I mean, with the pandemic and all?"

"But you're a licensed, private investigator. My fiancé is missing," Kirsten reasoned.

"True. Might be a bit tricky with the stay-at-home order, the pandemic bringing life as we know it to a halt. Might take some time, but I'll look into it."

"Well, looking into things is what you do better than anyone, from what I hear," Kirsten said.

"Well, you could say that," Hawk's intonation rose, and Kirsten noted pride in his voice. It was the kind of pride one has when speaking about something you love doing and you know you do it well. It was pride in service, rather than pride in self.

"I really appreciate it, Hawk," Kirsten said.

"Let me get back to you later this afternoon. I got a lawyer friend I'll get in touch with about any of the legal mumbo jumbo I need to know in regards to the pandemic." His voice reflected a heroic tone.

"Perfect. Thanks so much . . . Hawk? Should I call you 'Hawk'?"

"Yeah. Call me Hawk."

The hatch drew open with a long, haunting creak. Arian wasn't sleeping, merely suspended in a state of waking-death. Zombie mode, as he called it. He heard the familiar, ever so subtle slither of the Reptile as he descended the stairs. He felt the Reptile's signature dark energy draw near until it hovered over him. A plate touched down on the hard concrete with a clink. The thermometer gun pressed against his forehead and, a moment later, it pulled away. Then came the antiseptic spray. The Reptile sprayed it over him as per routine— starting with the face, a few sprays down his body, wetting his shirt, and then a generous spray over his hands. The Reptile removed the rope binding Arian's right wrist. Arian then lifted the blindfold and stripped away the duct tape. The process was so mechanical, so formal, like a contractual agreement. It almost felt professional. He felt a strange guilt, a nameless indebtedness—magnified by the Reptile's dark, towering presence—a strange sense that he should feel grateful? Grateful to eat, to breathe, to be alive?

"Bathroom?" the Reptile asked.

"No," Arian shook his head. *Did he just ask? Usually I have to beg to use it. Why the change of heart? More mind games?* Using the bathroom also felt like a privilege. When needed, he was taken to an old outhouse in the back of the house while the Reptile stood guard, shotgun in hand. Arian would usually use the bathroom at every possible opportunity. Just to get outside, to feel the open air, escape the darkness. But he didn't have the urge now, nor the energy.

Today's meal was a piece of stale, moldy bread, a boiled egg and a bowl of water. Arian reached the bread and wolfed it down. He didn't know why he always ate the bread first, but he did. Maybe it was a coating for the parched stomach, a net for everything else to be caught on. It was a teaser, an easing-into of one of life's greatest pleasures. Moldy bread became a delicacy, the *foie gras* of his dead world. Anything more, such as an egg, or milk, certainly wasn't expected and was icing on the cake. He knew too, that anything that could rid the smell, the taste of the duct tape clinging to his lips was God sent. He reached a shaky hand down and scarfed up the egg in one go, trying not to lock eyes with the Reptile, who stood looming over him like a dumb child, jaw hanging over his toes, head hunched below the ceiling.

He hated doing it, but it was part of the game; he had to ASK for the water bowl; he had to SHOW obedience—to beg like a dog. He was asked if he needed to use the bathroom, and now it was his turn to ASK. The Reptile always placed the water bowl on the concrete floor, just out of Arian's reach, just beyond the plate of food. *I have to be 'grateful,' have to show 'gratitude.' Grateful that I am fed, grateful that I am given water. Food, the lifeblood of us all is to be respected, cherished. Water is a privilege, not a right.*

They say we can go a few weeks without food, but only a few days without water. How many days can the Reptile go? Arian's mind was unanchored, taken adrift by a chaotic mental sea. *Does he eat? What if I went on a hunger strike? What if I never asked for water? Would he just stand there looking vapid, dumb, and psychotic like he does? Would he eventually prompt me? How long could he stand his own game?*

"Water," Arian said, pointing. The Reptile stared back, unmoving with those close-set eyes and open-mouthed slack-jaw. It was almost as if Arian didn't engage him, his face would just hang there forever.

"Please." Arian managed, holding back a kindling rage. The Reptile picked up the bowl and extended it. The game. The trickery. The psychological torture.

Go ahead, splash me, Arian thought. *Baptize me. I confess my sins a thousand times over, cleanse me, oh holy priest.* The Reptile stared dumbly back. Arian reached for the water. The Reptile didn't pull it away this time. He simply held it out, free for the taking. Arian took hold of it. *No games today, eh?* Arian's fingers twitched, shaking the bowl. Arian closed his eyes, and took a big gulp. He could feel the Reptile's eyes and dark energy oozing over him—a searing violation, a theft of dignity, a forced nakedness, a perverse exploitation of a human need. The act of sustaining oneself at the very edge of existence was not sexy. Arian opened his eyes, knowing the Reptile's tongue had done its darting thing. He felt it happen behind the seal and shield of his closed eyes.

The Reptile took the bowl and nodded, signaling the hanging chain. Arian raised his wrist and the Reptile re-tied it to the chain, re-did the blindfold, and duct taped his mouth. He took the bowl and plate, slithered back up the ladder, shutting the hatch behind him with a dull thud—returning Arian to the torturous limbo of a lightless void.

❧

"The US government made it official today, extending the countrywide self-quarantine and stay-at-home order to June 1st. The announcement came as WHO officials cautioned that in light of the growing number of infections and, taking some Western European countries as examples, those who rushed to lift their quarantines too early in hopes of revamping their economies, led to the deaths of hundreds of thousands; it is better to be safe than sorry. The announcement came from the steps of the White House as the country's daily death toll peaked at 1,200—with New York City remaining as the epicenter, and L.A. coming in as a close second. These major cities have by far contributed to the majority of the nation's deaths. Worldwide, the death toll from the deadly RABID-30 is now well over 2 million. The debate rages on as to the origin of the deadly virus, as conspiracy theorists claim it leaked from a lab, while WHO maintains it likely originated in a wet market in Central China. The search for patient zero is . . ."

Hawk changed the radio station and browsed until landing midway through Stevie Ray Vaughn's "Pride and Joy." He was sitting in his black Ford Crown Victoria, parked across the street from the FoodCORP warehouse where Arian used to work. He sat with one arm extended forward, wrist resting over the steering wheel, a cigarette burning between his fingers. In his other hand, resting over his thigh, was a photo of Arian.

He watched as FoodCORP drivers loaded groceries into trucks that were backed along a concrete dock. He imagined one of the drivers to be Arian, studying his movement, his timing, his methods. He glanced back down at the photo. Hawk was old school. He needed something in hand, something tangible to wrap his fingers, his mind around.

Hawk was in his late 50s. He had salt and pepper hair that fell down to his shoulders. His rugged good looks underscored a roguish appearance. He was like a 'bad boy' version of David Hasselhoff. He had black piercing eyes and a sharp downturned nose, like a beak. He had thin dry lips, a strong jawline and a thick brow. He didn't often wear sunglasses. He claimed they limited his razor sharp vision. He had light brown skin, from his mother's Native Cupeño roots. The Southern California tribe was subdivided into Coyote and Wildcat, of which he came from the Coyote. It is said they were expert trackers.

In the cold months he often wore a buffalo skin jacket, but today just a white t-shirt, and around his neck, a necklace with three bear claws, which was passed down from his mother on his eighteenth birthday. That was the year before she died of lung cancer. The necklace's provenance traced back to his mom's brother, also named 'Hawk.' He was among the greatest of their hunters and trackers.

This is where Hawk, the private eye, got his name, Steven Hawk MacConnell. Growing up, his friends called him Hawk. It used to bother him. He thought it sounded like someone from an old spaghetti western. But he didn't like the name Steven either. Steven was his father's name. He never understood why his mom named him after a man who ran out on them. Hawk supposed it was one way of attempting to keep someone close . . . relevant . . . or alive.

Hawk's father was Scottish-American, a fierce alcoholic. His father stormed through California's back country and tumbleweed towns, snatching those around him up in a whirlwind of troubles. Tall, lean and robust, his charms could quickly turn violent at a bottle's end, especially when disputes arose over unpaid debts. He usually didn't last a week or two per town, chasing one thrilling experience after the other. They say he was escaping gambling debts back east, that he borrowed money from the 'wrong people'.

He met Hawk's mother on a California Indian reservation, where she worked as a card-dealer at a casino. He disappeared shortly after running up debts and impregnating her. This elusive, mysterious man was the one person Hawk never successfully hunted down . . . at least, not yet. Rumors of his untimely death while escaping to Mexico came when Hawk was in his mid-twenties. Everything went quiet thereafter.

Did he make it across the border? Change his name? Or did his misdeeds finally catch up to him with blood as due payment? Hawk inherited his father's love of drinking and, coupled with his native blood, it was a perfect storm that led to more than his fair share of barroom brawls. He quit drinking six years ago, when a drunken motorcycle accident nearly destroyed his right leg. Metal rods and the miracle of modern medical science pieced it back together better than anyone could have hoped. But Hawk was done with the bottle, fights, and motorcycles. He sold his motorcycle and never stepped foot in a bar again.

Hawk was old school alright. He flicked his cigarette out of the window, pulled his eyes from the loading dock and unfolded a map over his lap. He ran his finger along the map, from the FoodCORP warehouse where Arian would start work, and up along I-15 to the first, then the second of the delivery points: Relocation Camp A1 and Relocation Camp A2. His finger lay over each camp for a moment, his mind like an anchor, combing the depths. He then reversed directions, tracing the route all the way back across the Mojave to the FoodCORP warehouse. He needed to feel the route, connect with it tangibly first, then . . . viscerally.

Hawk glanced up from the map as one of the drivers checked his watch and got into the truck. Hawk also glanced at the time on the dashboard. The driver pulled away from the loading dock and made a left, heading towards the on-ramp to Interstate 15.

Hawk set the map on the passenger seat beside him. He waited for the driver to pass, turned on the ignition and followed discreetly behind.

In his darkest hours, Arian thought of Kirsten, the bringer of light. He recalled her blonde-red hair and beautiful hazel eyes. Her tough, yet caring face held the responsibility of a committed, knowing sacrifice. It surprised Arian how much you think of people when you are stripped of everything, how important they become, not only for their love and support as family members and friends, but as symbols. Kirsten was his symbol of strength; she was the Lioness who hunted in the darkness. Darkness was her ally. And in Arian's dark world, she was the Huntress Queen.

Kirsten had an intricate tattoo of a lion that stretched across her upper back and shoulders, a holdover from her brief, but rebellious teenage years. The lion tattoo was baring ferocious canines. The mane spread from its face like the rays of the sun, cut into her skin, like tribal markings. But within the ferocity of its expression was a sense of justice and nobility.

Arian often thought about getting tattoos. He was a late-bloomer, late to develop, and late to express his individuality. He mostly just put his head down and did what he felt was right. He didn't discover the power of going his own way until his mid-twenties. That's when he quit his job as a team leader at a corporate marketing firm and started his worldly backpacking adventures. What he admired about Kirsten was her courage to express her individuality. She also knew what she wanted out of life—to help others. She discovered this at a fairly young age, whereas Arian floated from job to job, hobby to hobby, and country to country. The long-road of self-discovery stretched out ceaselessly before him, beckoning.

Like Kirsten, Arian was an only child. Growing up, his parents had daily squabbles over money. He internalized their frustrations and often saw himself as the cause of the family's financial problems. Their financial woes grew more serious as he got older. He became a people-pleaser, not wanting to create more worries for anyone. He shoved his personal needs to the side in order to serve others. He learned to cry in silence and to bleed in the shadows. He didn't ask for anything and was happy with very little. He didn't complain or fuss. In time, this only held him back, derailing his personal growth. He was strong-willed and determined, but was often unable to bestow much-needed self-love on himself.

Arian went to college, earning a place on the Dean's List every semester. But despite his hard work, he dropped out after a few years, uncertain that Business Administration was really for him. He took an entry position doing corporate marketing, and due to his dedication and hard work, was offered a management position.

Yet, at the office, he was often called 'soft' behind his back. Although he was mostly well-liked, others felt he was too accommodating and was ultimately holding the company back. Although he avoided confrontation, likening it to the drama he witnessed at home, he displayed a lot of heart, gave his everything and worked tirelessly. In this way, he often relieved much of the burden that fell on others shoulders. However, he lacked the confidence to stand up for his own needs and was often taken advantage of. He simply wasn't coldhearted enough for the corporate world.

The nine-to-five grew stale after a few years and he traded in the corporate office for the far-flung adventures of travel. He worked hard his final year and saved money, strapped on a backpack and began the restless wanderings that would occupy much of his late twenties. When he returned to the states after years of living and traveling overseas, he checked into a U.S. hospital with a nasty staph infection that he got after staying in an 18-bed hostel in Thailand.

That hospital is where he met Kirsten. He was vulnerable and worldly; she was strong and stable. They were opposites in many ways, but their chemistry was undeniable. They started dating soon thereafter. Arian had found what he'd been looking for—a reason to settle in one place, to dedicate himself wholeheartedly to someone, and a reason to start a family.

Family, Arian thought, *family*—suddenly a creaking whine came from above, pulling his attention to the present. The near-soundless slither, the dark vaporous energy strangled the air as the Reptile descended. Arian braced for the antiseptic spray. It came as usual, a demeaning ACT. He felt like an infectious rat. The pungent smell of the antiseptic engulfed the silence, and he stood at its mercy, wincing behind the blindfold. There was no sound of the plate touching down on the concrete floor.

Another layer to the game? The Reptile lifted Arian's blindfold. Arian winced under the hatch light as the Reptile untied his wrist.

Has death arrived? The Reptile undid Arian's other wrist, and his arm fell to his side as if it was prematurely pulled from a cast, not yet healed and forced into the world too soon.

"Aaaaah!" he screamed, curling over his knees. The Reptile pulled him up by the arm. Arian's legs stiffened and his knees buckled.

"Up!" The Reptile commanded, leading him to the stairs. Arian reached for the ladder. His shaking fingers struggled to grab hold. "Come on!" The Reptile nudged him from behind. When Arian finally made it to the top of the ladder, he saw the Pig, standing at the end of the hall, aiming the barrel of the shotgun. He did not dare look into those pig-like eyes. He preferred the eternal darkness of the dungeon than to lay his eyes on those inhumanly black orbs. In them, he saw a signed contract, written by the hand of death.

The Reptile led him down the hall. Arian squinted under the overhead light, unable to appreciate the luxury of being able to see. He felt pressure behind his watering eyes. He pushed on.

Come death, come, he thought. *And come swiftly. If not, I'll come for you and I'll take your fucking soul.*

"According to AT&T, the last ping from Arian's cell phone came from somewhere off I-15, in the middle of the desert," Hawk said into the phone.

"Off I-15, his work route?" Kirsten said.

"Yep. I'm headed out there today."

"Do you have the exact coordinates?"

"Yes, hold on," Hawk said. He then read the coordinates and Kirsten jotted them down.

"Got it. I'll do what I can on my end," Kirsten said.

Silence, brimming with what was unspoken, spread between them.

"Kirsten" Hawk said finally.

"Yeah?"

"Hang in there. These are wild times, anyone could get lost in the mix right now."

"I know."

"How're things at the hospital?"

"Uff, where do I start? I mean, it's a disaster. We're on the verge of collapse. We're running out of bed space and supplies. We're exhausted . . . but we're getting through it."

"Stay strong. You're the true heroes, fighting on the frontlines. We appreciate everything you do" Hawk said.

"Thanks Hawk, it means a lot."

"And remember to take care of YOURSELF, ok?" Hawk said.

"Yes, of course," she said, nodding.

"Oh, and Kirsten?" Hawk said after another long silence.

"Yes?"

"We're going to find your fiancé," he promised.

Hawk wasn't a talker; he didn't care much for words. Words were fancy, idyllic fluff that anyone could muster—a costume party, a grand ball, a beauty pageant. Words could too easily be pretentious or shallow. He was all-too familiar with the bombastic speech, rhetoric, and empty promises of politicians, religious leaders, and corporate heads. In turn, he had heard many a drunk spout their personal life philosophies too; spitting vitriol at their life-long mistreatment and misfortunes, while espousing brilliant remedies for society's ills, bestowing luminous wide-eyed wisdom to the masses from their elevated perch of booze-stained bar stools . . . never realizing that their victim mindset was their predicament, that their need to complain and subconscious love of suffering prevented their rise, their freedom, their happiness. Hawk himself had been that victim, that rambling drunk. And when he quit the bottle, he learned the true meaning of 'self-mastery.'

Words didn't impress him much, no. Hawk respected action. Action held power, not air, not fluff. Words should be used to move mountains, not paint skies. So, when Kirsten heard him say those words, "We're going to find your fiancé," she felt something deep inside reach up and ground her.

"Thanks. Talk to you soon." Kirsten said, and hung up. Kirsten was tough and, like Hawk, she felt that Arian was indeed out there somewhere. She knew that Arian was tough too. He wasn't a fighter in the traditional sense, not a stand-out athlete or particularly competitive, but he would give his all.

Hawk knew the desert. And he knew it wasn't meant for human habitation. Those who dared step foot over the barren land were pacing the slow, perilous walk of death. At any time, the sun could strip you of your lifeblood, sap away your water reserves, and sacrifice your flesh to the sun. The sun could leave you dry and weak, baked and shriveled like a dry raisin, or burn you to a crisp in a millisecond. The cacti, red-tailed hawks, iguana lizards, spiders, scorpions, and snakes were the chosen children of the sun—not man.

Hawk grew up on an Indian reservation with his mother near Death Valley. He knew you could lose a skyscraper out in that vast desert—that nothing was sacred; anything could be claimed or vanished into earth's parched belly. He was old school; He knew to trust his eyes, nose, and ears, and he was sure that he would find Arian—dead or alive.

Hawk sat in his Crown Victoria—on the shoulder off I-15 in the middle of the Mojave. He'd written the coordinates to Arian's missing cell phone on the white border of his map, and he noted the location on the map with a dark X. He studied the area like a general doing reconnaissance of enemy territory. He looked beyond his window at the thin white line of the horizon as I-15 stretched on as far as he could see. He imagined it going all the way to Nevada. He could smell the hot earth rising up to meet his nostrils and, with the medical mask resting below his chin, he stuck his nose out into the still, hot air and inhaled deeply. He looked back down at the big, darkly inked X on the map, then back up at the Interstate again. He turned on the ignition and drove on.

⌒

"That there's the kitchen." The Reptile pointed with his free hand, while leading Arian down the hall. Arian had grown accustomed to the stale, stagnate air of the basement, so that the sensation of air passing over his skin now sent shivers along his arms and neck.

Is it morning? Arian winced against the light showering down from an overhead bulb. *Afternoon?* Blinking back the tears from his watering eyes, he glanced up to find himself in the kitchen.

The small kitchen had a sink, countertop, stove and cabinets crammed against a wall. Pots and pans hung along the very top of the vine-and-leaf wallpaper and a strange black, short-legged spider, like a hidden camera from an alien world, hung in a cobweb in the corner where the wall met the ceiling. A stack of dishes sat in an inch of greasy sink water and the stench of rotting pipes crept up from some unknown source.

The Pig was leaning back in a wooden chair at the head of a dining table, opposite the kitchen. His belly rose and fell noticeably as he breathed, a nasally whistle accompanying his exhales. Between the greasy water and smell of rotting pipes, Arian could almost smell the Pig's breath. The Pig wasn't wearing a medical mask. Arian noted his dry, pink, pig-like skin, and crusty, sausage lips, which held a self-satisfied smirk. He had one leg propped up on a chair and rested one palm, face down over the table. Next to his downturned palm lay a loaded shotgun, inches from his meaty fingers.

That repulsive smirk, those dark penetrating eyes . . . vigilant and hovering in wait, like a drone ready to strike.

Arian felt the eyes over him and, when those meaty fingers tapped the table, he could almost feel it along his spine, as if strings gently pulled, as if to assert who is master and who is puppet.

The Reptile led Arian to the stack of dishes in the sink. "Wash" he said in a terse, dumb boy voice.

"Can I have some water?" Arian asked. The Reptile stared dumbly back, unmoving like a Royal guard.

"Please" Arian said, knowing the power of the word. *The game continues. Another layer peeled away.* The Reptile nodded towards a mug drying on a rack. Arian took it with a shaky hand, opened the knob of the faucet above the sink, and the sudden rush of water came like a vital force, tapped from some mystic life spring. Arian gulped the water down, almost forgetting that he was being watched, as always, by those strangely inhuman eyes. The water was fluoride heavy, and had the old-pipe taste he expected.

Would dirt taste good under these circumstances? he thought.

"Wash!" The Reptile's words fell like a butcher's knife, severing Arian's internal dialogue.

"Yes sir," Arian rolled up his sleeves. He spoke like a recruit answering a drill sergeant. *I can't believe I said that.*

The kitchen had the feel of an old shoe. Dirty, worn, and past its time, but homey. It was like a shoe that you thought your toe would blow right through at any moment or that the sole would detach with the next step, but somehow kept holding on.

Their eyes . . . their Goddamn eyes, Arian thought, scrubbing a dish with a dirty sponge. *I'm gonna gouge your eyeballs outta your fucking skulls.* He washed and hung dishes on the rack, limiting his attention to the task at hand. He felt like a horse with blinders on—as if using his peripheral vision was a breach of contract. The Pig's eyes would catch him if he wandered. They catch all. Anything outside of his task at hand was a privilege he hadn't been given.

That's right, a privilege. The voice of Auggie came to him. *You're a privileged little maid, doing dishes for King Pig and Prince Reptile.* Arian imagined that Auggie spoke in a low whisper, as if holding a secret meeting. *Next you'll be shining their shoes. You any good at giving foot massages? Ever hand-fed someone grapes? Fanned them with a palm leaf?*

Shut up, Arian shook his head. The Pig's eyes were over him, and the Reptile's dark vapory energy crept near. He tried not to think. His occasional subconscious thumbing of his engagement ring between dish scrubbing tempted mental escape. The thought of Kirsten only brought the paranoia that the Pig's eyes and the Reptile's dark energy would infiltrate his thoughts—infiltrate his private world.

I guess I will just die here, he thought. *After they wring-out every last drop of dignity I have, string me along in their mad little play, only to . . . eventually kill me?* That would be fair enough, as long as they didn't glimpse his personal life. In his mind, Kirsten was cocooned, a protective bubble sealed around her and their life together, protected by an impenetrable barrier of white light.

He tried to calm his shaking hands, disguise them with the dutiful movement of scrubbing. He knew that the shaking would be seen as a sign of weakness. They were weakening him by degrees, one chess move at a time . . . and observing it, clinically.

The Reptile slid over to a large pot on the stovetop and fired up a burner. The smell of propane filled the air. A moment later, the smell of sink water was cut by the smell of a thick, beefy broth.

Leftovers? Arian thought. Steam rose from the pot and rolled past his face, warming his nose and patchy whiskers. He could almost taste the beef, as the warm, homely stew teased his palate.

Are they actually going to feed me beef stew? Arian thought. *Is Auggie right, just like giving me water, is it a privilege? Am I 'privileged' to be out of the dungeon? Privileged to do dishes? Stew is my reward? My prize?*

Arian hung the last dish on the rack, realizing the dishes took him longer than it should have, and paranoia suddenly gripped him.

I was thinking too much, my actions too mechanical. The Reptile slid over to him.

"Sit!" The Reptile pointed at the dining room table, his finger the size of a carrot. The Pig lifted his palm and his first three fingers fell in a heavy, intent staccato over the table: "SIT-DOWN-NOW!" The rhythm commanded, the puppet master pulled at the strings.

Arian walked over and took a seat opposite the Pig. It was the precise chair the Pig's incredulous gaze guided him to. Arian dropped his eyes to the middle of the table, halfway between himself and the Pig. The table was hardwood, with sturdy, solid legs. A laminate table cloth was spread over the top, the kind Arian's grandma used to use. It had a classical Roman motif of Cupids, cornucopias and chalices repeated across it. There was an empty, foggy glass bowl centered on the table. Two squat, unlit candles sat to either side of it.

The Pig stared at Arian and said nothing. He seemed to swallow all of the room's light. Light from the uncovered bulb hanging directly over the table was in stark contrast to the deep shadows that fell over the wall behind him, obscuring what looked to be a hallway branching off from the opposite wall. The shadows fell in charcoal and ochres. Umbers played in the near-opaqueness. He was posed as royalty for a commissioned painting: "Napoleon I on his Imperial Throne" by Ingres.

Is this an act? Poised in a haughty recline, foot up on a chair, palm flat over the table, shotgun beside it. What is this, some kind of vulgar respectability? A narcissist King touting his own greatness? Am I supposed to be the painter? Commissioned to capture his likeness? No, I am much less than a painter in this sick play. I'm a simple peasant, allowed the privilege to eat with the king?

Yes, I told you. This is your 'privilege' the voice of Auggie jumped in. Arian batted his eyes, shutting Auggie away. Any show of weakness would only add to the curt smile across the Pig's fat lips.

They sat in silence, as the smell of the warming stew seemed to grow in intensity. Arian watched as the steam pooled in a loose spiral beneath the overhead light.

The Pig's smile widened, nearly imperceptibly—playing the silence, using the unsaid as leverage. The less that was said, the more space 'What ifs' would have to play, and the more psychological torture there was to sow. The Pig tapped his fingers on the table again—this time all four: the pointer, middle, ring, then pinky. Tick, tock, tick, tock. It kept time. It was neither patient nor impatient, neither passive nor aggressive—as if everything was in sync, and he was merely noting it.

"What do you want with me?" Arian postured up, like a cat raising its hair, not wanting to show fear, nor declare war, but to show he would put up a fight, was willing to die even, if that was the plan. The Pig's lips spread just visibly, for a mere, fleeting instant. He said nothing, but somehow seemed to shift the focus to his fingers, and the shotgun resting over the table.

The puppet master threatens to pull strings? Pull triggers? Or keep time? A signal that the game is his? The Reptile slithered to the table and set a bowl of stew in front of the Pig. He then served himself stew, and then set a plate with two pieces of stale bread, a single boiled egg and a glass of milk in front of Arian.

Milk again? But no stew for me? Privilege has levels to it, I guess. And so does the game.

The Reptile took his seat. The Pig pulled his foot off the chair, sat up, and interlaced his fingers. He bowed his head.

Is he going to say grace?

The Reptile also interlaced his fingers and bowed. Arian half closed his eyes; avoiding sight of the Reptile's lizard fingers, knowing their potential to instantly reach over and choke him to death.

The Pig began:

"Lord, thank you for our food.

By your Blessing we are fed.

We thank you Lord, for our daily Bread."

A prayer? You gotta be kidding me, Arian thought. He shot a glance at the Pig, noting his shut eyes and his erect, ostensibly reverent posture.

"Amen" the Pig said, then carefully unlaced his fingers and reached for the soup spoon. He kept his head low, eyes on the food, as if honoring the prayer. The Reptile did the same. Arian reluctantly reached for the bread on his plate. Bread first, as always. The bread, Lord. The bread.

Prayer? What a clumsy, farcical attempt to appear dignified, yet alone virtuous, Arian thought. The sound of slurping and the tin spoons scooping against the bowls played over the table, creating an unsettling sense of peace. After they finished eating, the Reptile rose from his seat, looked at Arian, nodded at the sink and said "Wash!"

Hawk eased off of the gas as a large 'Check Point' sign along the road came into focus. He drove past the sign, and pulled onto the shoulder. There were police and military vehicles parked along the highway and two armed guards standing at opposite sides of the entry gate to Relocation Camp A1.

An officer stepped over to Hawk's window, silencing a walkie-talkie with his thumb. Another, much larger officer with an automatic weapon across his chest stepped over to the passenger side window and stood guard. The officer with the walkie-talkie signaled for Hawk to roll down his window.

"Driver's License." The black-eyed, silver-eyebrowed officer said.

"Steven MacConnell. Private eye." Hawk extended his license. The officer took a hard look at it. He then motioned for Hawk to lower his facemask. Hawk did so, and the officer glanced back and forth between Hawk and the license.

"Put your mask back on," the officer said.

The officer probed the inside of the Ford with his black, discerning eyes. Hawk's rugged, rouge-like appearance painted him as an anti-hero from some B-rate 80's detective movie.

"What brings a Private eye all the way out here?" The officer asked dubiously.

"Missing Person."

"Missing Person?"

"Possible homicide," Hawk's eyes drew inward, solidifying into a bullet.

"This is high-level Quarantine," the officer barked.

"Here's my exemption from the County and State," Hawk produced a document.
The officer took it, stepped back and spoke into his walkie-talkie.

"L.A. County?" he said after some time.

"That's right."

"The missing person is Arian Guyd. FoodCORP and Pharmacy. Grocery Delivery," Hawk leaned forward, resting an elbow on the car door.

"FoodCORP?" The officer lifted an eyebrow. Hawk noded. The officer nodded curtly back. Hawk glanced up at the other officer standing guard beside his passenger side door, noting the automatic weapon across his barrel chest. His eyes were expressionless and hard, like eroded granite, slowly formed over time. He stood with his chin high, chest out. His pride of lineage showed in his formal, rigid bearing. The image of a Roman Legionnaire, Spartan or Mongol warrior could easily be superimposed over him. He was bred for this.

He caught Hawk's glance, and tightened his brow. Hawk shrugged, turned and looked up at the other officer, who was staring down at him. Hawk produced a photo of Arian, "Look familiar?" he said.

The officer scanned it.

"Look, we get suppliers coming in and out of the camp all week. Some of these drivers are new employees. Maybe only saw his face once or twice," the officer said.

"He comes here quite frequently according to FoodCORP records," Hawk said.

"They're all wearin' masks," the officer said.

Hawk looked back at him, his indrawn eyes unsatisfied.

"Maybe that baboon over there recognizes him," Hawk said, throwing a raised eyebrow at the officer with the automatic weapon.

"When was his last delivery?" the officer said.

"April 13th."

"That was some time ago."

"I've been calling, trying to get ahold . . ."

"Listen, if your Missing Person was here, he'd be on the list," the officer said, his words dropped to a deadpan. It was like a wall had begun to crumble and an ounce of diplomacy had slipped through the cracks.

Hawk's eyes drew open, pupils widened, his face softened, sensing movement.

"Johnson, bring me the check-in list for the last few weeks," the officer said into his walkie-talkie.

❧

Kirsten scrubbed her hands with a tenacity that bubbled up soap like a honeycomb of domed colonies. The colonies spread over germs and bacteria and, the rubbing of her palms, the wringing of her fingers and the soapy, slippery friction sealed the bacteria's fate with certain death. Death to RABID-30, death to giving in, death to giving up. Death to death. It was the third time she had washed her hands since coming home from the hospital that night. She showered, ate a light meal that she was barely able to finish and, immediately, the voices of her co-workers came to mind: *Are you ok? You eating enough? Sleeping well?*

That's the million-dollar question, she thought, as they all were overworked and pushed to extremes with the medical system on the verge of collapse. They suggested she take time off to deal with her missing fiancé. She mostly refused. When they occasionally forced her to take a few days off, the isolation and endless milling about only inflamed the incessant 'What ifs,' making things infinitely worse.

Arian hated when Kirsten speculated about the 'What ifs.' She inherited this habit from her mother. Her mom was a bit of a worry-wart. But she also inherited her intelligence and strength from her mom. No, she couldn't just sit at home and go crazy, worrying about Arian. She preferred to be on the front lines, saving lives alongside her fellow nurses, medical staff, and doctors . . . saving lives . . . by pushing to flatten the curve . . . saving lives by doing what she believed in most—helping people . . . and potentially saving the life of her fiancé by placing nagging phone calls to the police department during her lunch breaks . . . and saving lives by . . . keeping her damn hands clean.

She turned off the faucet and ran a rag over her hands. The skin of her hands was peeling, frail, white, and over scrubbed. She thumbed her engagement ring, which she refused to remove. They agreed not to take their rings off unless it was absolutely necessary. It wasn't for anyone else, it wasn't for show. It was their bond, a symbol of their strength, their solidarity. The promise to be in the fight together. *We're in this together, just like all of humanity fighting against this damn virus,* she thought.

They had not yet flattened the curve; death tolls were still on the rise, to the tune of nearly 1,300 a day in the state alone. There were talks of extending the quarantine for another two weeks. Opposition had arisen over the damage being done to the economy; without easing it back open and lifting the quarantine by degrees, the entire world would plummet into the worst economic depression history has ever known.

Extreme Conservative groups were breaking Stay-At-Home orders and coming out of their homes to protest at state capitals. They argued that the orders were in violation of their constitutional rights. These protests were especially strong in the South and Midwest. New York was still the worst, in terms of the number of daily cases and L.A. wasn't too far behind. They quickly became poster children of what NOT to do.

"Delayed Response: Why NY and L.A. are in Big Trouble" Kirsten recalled a news headline. The virus 'what ifs' continued to torment her throughout the day, especially at work. But when she got home, the 'what ifs' were mostly about Arian.

That night, while lying in bed, she grabbed her phone from the nightstand and opened a text from Hawk.

"On the trail. Hope you're well. Let's talk tomorrow," it said. His messages were always terse. He didn't like texting much and preferred to talk over the phone or in person. She did too. Hearing Hawk's voice made her feel closer to Arian somehow. Hawk became her other leg in the fight. His unflagging belief that Arian would be found became their bond. She had no choice but to join him in the war cry.

Whereas the authorities put out a half-assed search, strapped for resources or whatever, there would be nothing half-assed with me, Kirsten thought. *Nor Arian. He was never the best. But he always tried.*

☙

The Moon cast its shadow over the Mojave, creeping ever-so slowly across the sky, and the sun settled down with an aura of ancient, ritualistic calm—putting its light to bed and yielding the kingdom to the nocturnal creatures of night. This was the time of a shift change, a changing of the guard. It was a flip of the coin, a desert tango—each partner equal but operating in different dimensions of space-time. It was the awakening of yin and sleeping of yang. As darkness fell and the sand cooled, the patrons of the night answered the call to the hunt.

Hawk walked along the shoulder of Interstate-15, chasing the last of the sun rays as they bent into a fantastic orange finality over the rim of the earth. He had walked this path twice before, which brought him roughly within the coordinates of Arian's cellphone. With the telephone towers spaced so far across the desert, it was difficult to know exactly where the phone was last. Assuming it was on Arian when the last ping was picked up, his phone, maybe his truck, and even Arian himself, could be within a stone's throw of the coordinates.

Hawk smelled the air. He scanned the ground, stepping with a slight limp, carefully placing each step as if he were a guest on the earth. The hunt was his meditation. Silenced thought, regulated breath. His ears perked up like a cat waiting for the mighty desert to speak. He stopped suddenly, reached down and ran his finger in the sandy rock along the Interstate. He brought it to his beak-like nose, and continued on.

He followed along a stretch of wire fencing that ran along the Interstate for miles. The fence line was broken only by unused farm roads. He stepped over, rested his arms on the sun-beat fencing and took in the panorama of rock, cottontop and foxtail cacti, and the countless grains of sand—spread as if from a liberal hand, painting earth's surface with the sands of time. This sand covered all, claimed all, and caused the very hand of time to stop. The mountains were a distant silhouette, bordering the backdrop in a veil of deep silk.

Hawk's eyes came finally to the ruins of an old farm road, stemming off the Interstate, and dispersing into a labyrinth of rock and shrub beyond. It was barely noticeable . . . long forgotten. Its initial form had given way to the chaotic beauty of nature. He studied the old road for some time, then nodded finally, as if ending a dialogue between worldly forces. He continued along the fence line to the entrance of the old road.

Before taking the road, he kneeled down on one knee and ran his finger along the gravelly mix of pavement and sand tapering down from the Interstate. He brought it to his nose, sparking a memory of a body he'd encountered lying face down on the desert floor two days before. Another No Man's Land suicide; brains scattered across the rock and dust, a fallen 9 mm pistol next to a pale, desperate hand. An empty whisky bottle near the stiff, outstretched fingers of the other. A father, a brother, a son—another nameless victim claimed by the pandemic. Another feast for the turkey vultures, another sacrifice to the Sun God. He shook his head, and the memory left him. He exhaled long and slow and rose to his feet. He narrowed his eyes over the once-road, then followed it into the darkness.

Is that what they do? Steal groceries, kidnap, imprison and starve people only to make them their personal house maids? Auggie was fast-becoming Arian's least favorite person . . . or imagined person, rather. But he needed someone to talk to. Arian was down on his knees, his body hanging in the darkness. His knees were calloused and his arms stiff and drained of blood. His shoulders were locked into place, a numb he'd nearly grown accustomed to. That is, until his knees could no longer take it anymore, and he'd switch to standing. He would also go into a semi-squat between kneeling and standing. It was these three positions that provided the least discomfort and pain. It was his daily math equation, his daily task of pain management, to be on the positive side of the ratio. It was his personal death-dance of attrition.

And why the blindfold? Auggie wasn't done. *I mean, you've seen the basement, what is to see of it anyway. A simple, dark dungeon. Nothing sophisticated about it. No windows or doors. Just four concrete walls and the hatch above. I guess that's what makes it so damn spooky. And the kitchen, wow. They let you eat at the table! Let you SEE the kitchen, the table. So why keep you blindfolded down here? Part of their sick game, isn't it?*

Auggie now sounded like one of Arian's College professors, Dr. Merrick. That's it. Auggie was Dr. Merrick, waxing philosophical on the Stoics. Long tedious, pedantic lectures on Marcus Aurelius and his Meditations. Arian found Stoic philosophy interesting, actually. But Dr. Merrick could really drag out a lecture with that raspy voice of his.

Auggie was generally less pedantic, more analytical and suspicious. He was a constant digger. Arian knew he would really enjoy unraveling the psychological puzzle Arian was in. And at times, when not exaggerating things, Auggie's sharp mind could be quite an asset. His mind was a mix of Psych 101 and Philosophy 101 . . . and a dash of Criminology. When Auggie lectured, Arian usually didn't mind so much . . . until he did. Then Auggie quickly would become Arian's least favorite person again. Since there was no TV, no radio, or internet, Auggie's imagined voice would have to do.

If they were gonna kill ya, they would've done it already, right? Auggie went on. *Actually, if they are as diabolical and cunning as they seem—Well, at least the Pig seems to be diabolical and cunning. The Reptile? Well, he's just a sick, intimidating imbecile, isn't he? What great names you have for 'em, eh? The 'Pig' and 'Reptile?' What is this, 'Animal Farm?' Well, I digress. My point is . . .* Arian pictured Auggie rubbing the stubble of his chin, his discriminate, inquisitive eyes behind his thin-rimmed glasses, excitedly swimming in a soup of his own mind-matrix. A self-perpetuating 'what if' machine of endless conspiratorial possibility.

I guess the 'what ifs' get us all from time to time, Arian thought.

Maybe you aren't the first person they've kidnapped. I mean, you noticed yourself that the Pig had a certain look in his eyes, like he was following a script. Look how he was poised at the table yesterday. He and the Reptile work in tandem, setting traps. A smooth operation free of hiccups or the trademark sloppiness of a maiden voyage. Just another day at the office. It certainly wasn't their first rodeo . . .

Arian shook his head, pushing Auggie away. *Since Auggie is merely a memory, an imagined conversation or more accurately, what I imagine Auggie to be saying, it is not Auggie who is speaking at all, but me, projecting my own thoughts of Auggie onto what I would imagine him to say. A byproduct of insanity? Or a defense mechanism against insanity?*

Auggie continued: *Why waste food and resources on you if they plan to kill you? Wouldn't they just kill you right away? Their motive being the food and medicine you had on your truck. The need for survival, the need for such basic necessities during the pandemic. People are looting stores and hoarding supplies. So why kidnap you? Unless that was part of the plan all along? Aside from the groceries, what do you contribute? Are you worth your daily bread as a dishwasher?*

Daily bread? Arian began to smile at the innocuous pun, then snuffed it out—a half-birthed expression of joy. *The utter ridiculousness, the absurdity. Entertainment? None of this is funny. This is insanity.*

Just then he heard the hatch open, and the sudden glow of yellow-orange light washed over his face and blindfold, slanting in from above. The approaching slither. The effortless glide. The Reptile walked on air.

Back up to the kitchen? More dishes and the exclusive privilege to eat with them? He felt the dark energy of the Reptile approaching. Then came the sound of a plate touching down on the concrete.

Food?

The Reptile tested Arian's temperature with the thermometer gun, and sprayed Arian with antiseptic. He then un-tied his right wrist, freeing it from its ruthless paternity; the chains of the Godhead. His arm fell stiffly and excruciating pain shot from his arm into his neck and shoulder. He bucked forward as if jolted by electricity, screaming into the muffled wall of the duct tape. He knelt in pain for some time, his arm regaining lifeblood, feeling. The Reptile pulled the blindfold up to Arian's forehead, freeing his eyes.

The privilege of seeing, he thought, echoing Auggie's sentiments. The Reptile then stripped the duct tape away from his mouth.

The privilege of eating, Auggie chimed in.

Shut up Auggie, Arian eyed the plate which sat at his feet on the concrete. It had two slices of stale bread.

No dishwashing for me today, Arian thought. *No meal at the table. No basking in the presence of royalty.* Arian reached for the bread, and scarfed it down.

"Water. Please," Arian said.
The Reptile reached for the water bowl, that simple cross-eyed, boyish look on his face. His stooping shoulders, disheveled red hair, long face and slack-jaw loomed over, seeding phobias. The Reptile held out the water bowl with his incredibly large hands with their scaly, lizard-like skin.

The game continues. There must be some form of psychological torture, must be some continued mind fuck. Do I get my shower today? Arian thought. He reached a trembling hand for the water bowl. The Reptile extended it. Just as Arian's hand came within a few inches, the Reptile pulled the bowl back, then rocked it forward, splashing Arian in the face. Arian jerked back. He shut his eyes and drew a deep breath as the water ran down his forehead and cheeks.

It's been two days. I think it has, at least. I almost missed the feeling.

Hawk was parked along the shoulder of Interstate-15, parallel to the fence and the old farm road that stretched off into the distance. He wiped mucus from the corner of his eyes and pulled his ringing cell phone to his ear; "Hello?"

"Hawk?" Kirsten said.

"Yeah . . . Yeah, I'm here," Hawk said with a yawn.

"Sorry, did I wake you?" Kirsten said, glancing at a clock on the wall. It read: 12:37 PM.

"I'm glad you called," Hawk pulled the car seat forward and sat up. He grabbed his Stetson from the passenger seat, which sat over an open fold-out map, and put it on. It cut back the piercing sun slanting in from beyond the window.

"Kirsten, how are you?"

"I'm ok . . . working a lot, as you can imagine. Talking to my parents. Talking to Arian's parents too. They're worried shitless."

"I can imagine . . . and how are YOU?" Hawk reiterated.

"Hanging in there," she said.

"Look, he's out there, and we'll find him," Hawk promised.

"The police aren't doing a damn thing."

"Don't expect much from them. I'm sure they've got their hands full."

"Christ."

Hawk cleared his throat; there was business to get down to; there was yet juice to be squeezed from the lemon.

"Listen. The last delivery Arian made was to Relocation Camp A1, on April 13th. There is no record he ever made it to Camp A2 that day."

"No record?"

"Neither FoodCORP nor Camp A2 has a record for that day. He must have disappeared before he got to Relocation Camp A2, just as we suspected."

"I see," Kirsten said.

"His last known cell phone coordinates are between Camps, which isn't hard to imagine, given the distance. Judging by his work record, he normally leaves Camp A1 around 15:30 and makes it to Camp A2 by 18:00, so it means he must have disappeared sometime in between.

"It makes sense, yes," Kirsten said.

"So he still would have had a decent load of groceries and medicine at the time," Hawk said.

"Right. Probably half the truck was full."

"Exactly. As you know, people have been clearing out the aisles at supermarkets, panic-buying," Hawk said.

"You think someone killed him for supplies?"

"No. That's not what I'm getting at. It wouldn't be worth it. Most likely, he was robbed. Whoever did this went after the groceries and medicine. They would have snatched up any medical masks, gloves, antiseptics, or vitamins. Maybe stole the truck, even."

"But what about Arian, someone could have hurt him or left him for dead. There's endless desert out there."

"Maybe . . . or maybe they kidnapped him."

"But with the fear of catching the virus, why would anyone want to risk it?" Kirsten reasoned.

"Your fiancé is young and healthy—not high-risk. As a carrier, yes, more so. But FoodCORP as well as the Camps take all necessary precautions and have strict controls," Hawk said. He wasn't showing any symptoms, was he?"

"Well no . . ." Kirsten said.

"In any case, I think he's out there."

"So my fiancé is held hostage out in the middle of the desert somewhere, is that it?"

"I get the feeling he's out there, yes."

"A feeling?"

"Call it a hunch."

"A hunch? Hawk, my fiancé could be dead! He's been missing for weeks!"

"What I'm saying is that there's hope. Listen. He could have crossed into Nevada. It wasn't part of his route, but Camp A2 isn't far from the border. The Missing Person's report has been filed."

"But it's not a missing person, it's a possible . . . homicide," Kirsten stuttered.

"I'm going to follow-up with the Highway Patrol and the Sheriff's office later today."

"Hawk, I know you're good at what you do . . . but I'm not sure any of this makes a whole lot of sense to me right now," Kirsten rubbed her forehead with the thumb and pointer finger of her free hand.

"Look. I've always trusted my gut. That's been the basis of my whole career. The mind can only take you so far. The gut goes deeper. That's the best I can explain it."

There was a long silence between them.

"And my gut tells me your fiancé is out there," Hawk said finally. He's out there and I'm going to find him."

"Okay."

"Listen, there are some old farm roads, barely visible from the Interstate. All within a relatively short drive of Arian's cell phone coordinates. He could have sought shelter at one of those old ranches or farms. I've been tracking them. I'm headed over to another one now." Another silence drew out between them, even, unhurried.

"I gotta get back to work," Kirsten said.

"Me too" Hawk said, his eyes blinking against the eye mucus, the previous night of tracking still heavy over him.

"Kirsten," Hawk said.

"Yes?" her attention was pulling back to her work.

"We'll find him," Hawk said.

"I gotta go," Kirsten said.

"Ok. Talk to you soon." Hawk pulled the phone from his ear.

"Hawk, wait!" Kirsten said.

"Yeah?"

"Thanks," Kirsten said.

"Take care of yourself, now," Hawk said.

Hawk set his phone on the center console. He stretched back against the seat, pushing off the floorboards with his feet and arched his back, releasing a full body yawn, taking in the sun through the window. The sun bore down, heating the car like a tin can. Its heat was a kind of double-edged sword, oppressive yet revitalizing, as if it were up to the person to choose how to take it. It warmed his skin and a subtle, almost subliminal excitement permeated the desert air.

Hawk seldom expressed excitement or emotion. He said what he meant, and he did what he said. Emotions were those innate feelings, those highs and lows, fluctuations that give life its color, its character. But he preferred to keep them on an even keel. A homeostatic system of checks and balances of the mind, body and spirit too. It was so each played as an equal partner, no one ran off into its own insistent world. He respected the full range of human emotions just as he respected the abilities of the mind, but everything in its place, everything in its time. He knew now was the time of his "gut." It wasn't a feeling or an emotion. It was a sense. It commanded its own logic, had its own, oftentimes incessant reasoning.

He'll save the celebrations until it's all said and done—when all that he said and promised was done. He'll hedge his bets until then. After the last few days of tracking desert roads and wandering late into the night, only to fruitlessly return to his car and fall to a dead sleep, with throbbing pain in his bum leg, his heavy eyes and the wrenching feeling in his gut told him that he was close.

As before, there was a stack of dishes waiting for Arian in the kitchen sink—to begin the ACT. After washing them, Arian found himself sitting with the Pig and Reptile at the dining table. The Pig had the same, pretentiously regal poise as before, the Reptile the same docile subservience.

Is it morning or afternoon? Arian pondered. *It can't be evening yet, no. It must be early afternoon, judging by the amount of natural light making its way in. Besides, it's still too hot to be evening.*

The house was surprisingly comfortable, given there was no fan or air conditioning. His home was a dark box that he was blind to. He was blind to a blind world, subjected to darkness to drown-out the darkness. How poetic.

He chewed a piece of stale bread. He'd grown accustomed to its hardened flakiness—crystalized air with hints of mold. The Pig and Reptile had big slabs of bloody steak and a side of beans on their plates.

Steak? Arian thought. *What a luxury. And on such a presumably hot day in . . . early May?* Temps were on the rise before he got . . . kidnapped.

Steak, really? Was it all for show? All part of the ACT? The first time he had the 'privilege' to eat at the table, it was leftover soup. Now the jump to steak? The mind fuck continues. The sinister playstrings of the trickster. His mind wandered.

Ah yes, the same. He was thinking about how things were the same as his first 'privileged' meal, yet other things such as the steak, were noticeably 'different'.

The pretense, the posing. The act. ACT TWO. King Pig and Prince Reptile. Prince Reptile, yes, that's it. The tall red-headed imbecile . . . prince. He is dark, powerful . . . dangerous. Stupidity and power combine to be one of the most frightening things imaginable. The same, yes. Things are more or less the same as before, aside from the white, embroidered cross on the wall, hanging just above the Pig's head. Did I not notice that before? The same black shadows and earthy colors haunt the back wall behind him, just as before. But I don't remember seeing that cross. I would have noticed it before. It hangs on the wall so innocuously, so perfectly placed over the Pig's head from my point of view, framing him . . . piously. A halo. The deified Christian Pig King. The game. The ACT. Oh, yes, and what did the Pig say for prayer today? Arian thought for a moment, drawing the words in from some distant, gelatinous ooze, his chewing working his memory like a rotor, churning the thought-soil. Arian recalled:

"Thank you Lord for our daily bread,
For we are your Children,
Your Family,

Family, oh Lord

For whom you graciously provide love and bread."

How the Pig emphasized the word 'Family'. Subtly inflected, was it a cunning attempt to endear—an emotional snare-trap? The situation is anything but familial. And 'bread?' Contrived, deceptive, sick. Am I being 'rited' into the family? Is this my proverbial baptism? First prisoner, then housemaid, now . . . family? Could the Reptile be the Pig's brother? Could it be? Despite the lack of resemblance? Age wise, it could be possible. Or cousins? Related somehow, yes that's plausible. Family, Arian repeated in his mind. *Their 'family' is sick. This is sick. Inhuman. Mind-fuckers.* He tore a piece of bread with his teeth and chewed it. *Sick, sick, sick. Or is it me that is insane?*

He expected Auggie to butt in with his ceaseless narrative, take his cue, as Auggie was never gun-shy about speaking his mind. *The ceaselessly outspoken, just come-out -and-say-it and take no prisoners Auggie. Good 'ol conspiratorial Auggie. Take no prisoners. Jesus, how apropos. Apropos, but not funny. Oh, and did you have to say 'Jesus?' Damn. I must be going batty,* Arian thought.

But Auggie didn't take his cue, didn't say a word. Perhaps the sane part of Arian's mind refused to allow such simple wordplays or entertainments into the already surreal.

Perhaps madness is what they want. The drill sergeant sees how much a cadet can take until he breaks. Build 'em up and break 'em down. No, there can be no fun 'n games in this madness. Otherwise I'll be as sick as them, he thought.

Arian found himself back in the moment, chewing slowly and deliberately, trying to keep pace with the Pig and Reptile. He didn't want to outpace them and sit in the awkward silence of staring at an empty plate while they continued to eat. And he didn't want to give the Pig any opportunity to read his thoughts, although he could sense his ear at the door, his dark eyes forever peering through the proverbial peep-hole.

They ate with just the sound of the steak knives and forks clinking against the plates and the visceral rumblings of digestion. The Pig kept his head somewhat bowed as he ate. *Feigning humility?* His eyes ostensibly off Arian, but still 'watching.' The Pig's psychic camera was not just watching, but studying, taking notes. And of course, the loaded shotgun was laid across the table with the barrel angled toward Arian. It was just out of Arian's reach. Even if Arian stood up and reached across the table, he would barely lay fingertips on the tip of the barrel.

Everything is done so purposefully, everything carefully measured. The Puppet Master is at the controls. The Pig wouldn't stand a chance without that damn gun . . . but the Reptile is deceptively quick and unbelievably strong.

*The way he unloaded the groceries from my truck was nothing short of Herculean. He did it quickly and without breaking a sweat. But reptiles don't sweat, do they? Besides, even if I did manage to grab the gun, I don't know how to shoot. But could I fake it? Could I at least threaten with it? At close range I would have at least a 'puncher's chance.' C'mon, anyone can shoot a damn gun. It can't be that hard, right? Naw, it wouldn't be worth it. **Stop it. He'll hear you.*** Arian slammed his thoughts away like a desk drawer, a resonant finality echoing in his mind.

The Pig cut a piece of steak, severing the bloody fibers with the edge of his knife. With the sawing motion of the knife's teeth came a hint of death, ritual death. And sacrifice? The Reptile reached over for Arian's plate. Arian froze, a bolus of soggy, semi-chewed bread in his mouth. The Reptile nimbly swept up the plate and extended it over to the Pig. The Pig slapped down a cut piece of steak onto Arian's plate, then the Reptile set it back in front of Arian, all in a single swoop. Arian swallowed hard, eyeing the cut of steak.

"EAT" the Reptile said, sitting down to his steak and beans. The Pig looked on like a teacher, attentive to every detail, knowing every one of his student's weak points.

Steak? What a privilege. The plot twists of the mentally ill. It's a trap. But I can't refuse. I can't show that I'm on to the game. And what would refusal do anyway? Starve myself further? Plunge myself deeper into atrophy? I mustn't show resistance. It won't serve me now. And the steak smells so damn good! The smell of seasoned, savory beef rose to his nose. *Grateful, I must appear grateful.*

The smell conjured up the exotic, the forbidden. Something primitive came alive in him, and he reached down with both hands and bit into the steak, squeezing blood into his mouth like from a sponge. He closed his eyes and ripped into the fibers, its blood an unnamable seductress. He was a wolf devouring a carcass.

"You're married?" The Pig said.

Arian looked up with wolf's eyes. The Pig smirked, not so much at his question, which was more like a statement, than at the question's ensnarement.

A trap, I knew it. And All it took was a cut of steak? Arian centered his wolf's eyes. *The King wants you to enjoy, and for you to know that he knows you are enjoying. And that he can interrupt you any time he pleases. The Puppet Master reveals his strings,* Arian thought.

The Pig's smirk widened. His gaze lingered, catching Arian's wolf's eyes. Arian held ground and he chewed on.

"No," Arian said finally.

"The ring" the Pig said, this time more like a question than a statement. Arian glanced at his hands, which each held an end of the steak. His fingers were naked; the ring was in his pocket. *Shit. Of course he must have seen it. The gall to speak of my ring? My engagement, my world, my Kirsten?!*

Arian's stomach churned, gas burned up into his throat and reddened his face. His veins pulsed, his heart pumped. He let out a long, silent exhale, steam escaping his pores. He lowered his wolf's eyes and bit into the steak, imagining his teeth tearing at the Pig's flesh. He imagined gouging out those sick, dark eyes with his thumb. He sat up, his spine straightening, his shoulders squared, he felt a head rush of blood—a wolf ready to pounce. Suddenly his logical mind kicked in, like a referee separating emotion and logic on opposite sides of a boxing ring. The two sides of his brain jockeyed for position. Logic overcame emotion, and was set to diffuse the bomb. The Pig's eyes flickered over a wide smirk.

"No? I could have sworn you were wearing a ring," the Pig said facetiously. Arian stared back, his wolf's eyes in retreat, defenses drawn. Silence spread between them like a thick mist.

"Good steak?" The Pig changed the subject, pocketing the former subject as a psychological victory. The Pig's willingness to bring up the ring—to delve into Arian's personal life—was a violation. It crossed the line. But conversely, Arian noted the Pig's willingness to drop it.

Pick your battles, Auggie told him. *You gotta say something. Play into the game a bit. If you show that you're offended, he has you. Don't let him push your buttons man! Outbursts of anger or aggression will do nothing. You gotta be smarter than that.*

Damn it, you're right, Arian cleared his mouth with a swish of his tongue.

"Yes," he said at last, his wolf eyes gone. The Pig retreated by degrees, calling off the troops. Satisfaction showed in a narrowing, near-imperceptible flicker of his eyes. He spooned up beans from his plate and chewed piggishly. The Reptile ate quietly, seemingly uninvolved in the ACT. Or merely playing his part? Eating was the one time when the Reptile's dark energy settled . . . a muted wispy aura at his side like a servant.

Interestingly enough, as eating seemed all too natural for the gluttonous Pig, it was the opposite for the Reptile. The Pig had the gut and meaty extremities to show, the Reptile much taller and lean. The Pig also always took twice the amount of servings. When the Reptile ate, it was an uneventful, straight-forward act of biological necessity. Like the need to sleep or urinate, he didn't seem to particularly enjoy it, just heeded the call. It was a series of empty, obligatory motions. Would steak or stale bread be all the same to him?

"Did you enjoy the steak?" The Pig stole the focus back.

"Yes," Arian said.

"Protein is the cornerstone, water our lifeblood," the Pig eyed the glass of water by Arian's side.

"Y-e-s." Arian elongated the word, as if to say 'What are you getting at?"

"That's what's wrong with the world today. We've forgotten how to appreciate, to value even the simplest of things." The Pig now sounded erudite.

"Right," Arian played along. *Did he just shed his country accent?*

The Pig settled into his seat like an uncle about to share a story.

"My family grew up puttin' our hands to the soil, breakin' our backs to put food on the table," he said. He swiped his lips and continued: "My father and his father. My great, great grandparents were farmers goin' generations back. 'Ol' mud hands,' they used to call 'em. Now 'rednecks of the west'. Patience came with the land. Patience came at your own hand, sowing the seed, reaping the harvest. The clock was the LAND'S clock. The natural cycles, changes of seasons. The birds, the insects, the amount of moisture in the soil can tell ya what time of day it is, what season it is. We don't need a wrist watch to tell us when the sun is comin' up or settlin' down. We don't need no damn Google to tell us when, what, where or how to do things. We can see it, smell it, touch it, feel it. We use our senses, that's right, the five senses. The use of which, one may call common sense, which unfortunately, is becoming increasingly less common. But there just ain't no sense in outpacing ourselves. The world is moving too damn fast. Y'all want it all NOW. We all got 24 hours in a day. Goin' faster ain't gonna make the sun come up any sooner. It sure as hell ain't gonna make 'em crops grow any faster. We've lost touch with the land, the rhythm, timing—how to listen to it, care for it, love it, live in alignment with it. And this virus, this pandemic is just a way of God punishin' us."

The Pig turned and looked off into the distance, waxing philosophically. The embroidered cross on the wall behind him seemed to emphasize his Christian notions. Arian knew he was in for it, and his feedback wasn't solicited. The dark priest was at the podium, reading his manifesto. Shut up and take notes.

"Sweatshops springing up all over third-world countries, exploiting the poor and uneducated, destroying the land and poisoning the water. Proliferating cheaply-produced junk we don't need. Plastic trinkets and shiny lil' accessories destined for landfills and 'plastic islands.' Insignificant little trinkets just for you--at the expense of habitats and ecosystems near and far.

Air so polluted, some countries advise citizens to stay indoors for days at a time. People dyin' of every type of cancer imaginable. Technology does improve our lives, to some degree, of course. But where do we draw the line? More than 70% of the world's animal species are extinct! Continued deforestation of the Amazon and the Indonesian forests for what, hamburgers and palm oil? All the while we focus on infinite economic growth on a finite planet? It just don't make no sense. What are our plans, REALLY, to tackle climate change? A series of empty promises on behalf of our world leaders clearly isn't enough. When are we gonna step back and realize the very real consequences of living in disharmony with the planet?"

What? The gluttonous, redneck Pig is now a well-spoken intellectual? Arian held the surprise from showing on his face.

"All species compete for survival. Survival of the fittest as they say, natural selection. But are we really as dumb as the so-called dinosaurs that ate themselves to extinction? Or was it a comet that wiped 'em out? Or did God punish them for their simplicity and ignorance? Are we really all that more evolved than dinosaurs? Look at what we do? We shit in our own backyard. We destroy the only planet we got. The Bible never made no mention of no dinosaurs anyway. But the Gospel of Matthew certainly mentions these End Times we're livin' in. Matthew 24:29: After the tribulation of those days the sun will be darkened, and the moon will not give its light, and the stars will fall from the sky, and the powers of the heavens will be shaken.'" The Pig drew another breath, as if part of the sermon.

Arian needed a breath too. Too many thoughts rushed in— how the cross was conveniently placed on the wall during their second meal together, the Pig's 'prayers' before meals, the long diatribe.

Interestingly enough, neither the Pig nor Reptile wore crosses around their necks or in any other way appeared outwardly Christian.

Arian thought: *Am I really being held hostage by a luddite Philosopher King, espousing deeply-seated Conservative Christian rhetoric?*

I need to feign interest. Showing disinterest won't get me any closer to why I'm here, what their end game is, and how I can survive it. The more information I gather, the better. Before their master plan fully unfolds. The Puppet Master's final ACT? The show must go on, I suppose.

"Ya see, the old world is dying," The Pig went on: "And the new world is racing off to an early grave. Everythin' is moving so fast. Our values have been crushed beneath the maw of a technological tsunami—the highly addictive juggernauts—The internet, Netflix and TV—a world of information at your fingertips! Social media is a popularity contest bereft of a mortal soul, a superficial ooze melting away our values . . . the purveyor of moral decay, a false world devoid of humanity. How many times have you seen a room full of people more engaged with their phones than with each other? People seem to prefer interacting in the digital world more than in the real one.

Are people no longer human? Pimping themselves out as products in a society increasingly more interested in emojis and avatars—sold to the highest . . . or should I say, LOWEST bidder? News, commercials and targeted advertising bombard you every second of every day, arresting your attention, pulling you into a whirlpool of meaningless, shallow distraction. Memes and GIFs leap out in desperation for mere seconds of your precious, ever-withering attention-span. The attention-grab is the cash-grab. Now, now, NOW. Ain't no value given to the past. The latest distraction is so catchy, so short-lived, seizing yer attention ever so briefly, then passing within seconds only to be replaced by the next triviality. So fast, your lives rush on, off into nothing and for naught. What's new, what's trending? What's going viral? What does the latest Algorithm have for me--Now? Yer multitasking, tryin' ta keep up with multi-distractions. Yet ya lack satisfaction. Are we witnessing the unsustainability of hyper-stimulation? The perpetual pleasure-chase to nowhere? Fast-food, instant gratification, bottomless sexual appetites--yer a hamster, continuously running on a wheel.

Manipulated news media, misinformation campaigns, and propaganda are effectively triggering highly emotive, fear-based responses that are spinning the world out of control. Society has become distracted and reactive, rather than calm and collected. In-depth study and research is replaced with browsing, posting and sharing. A quick glance, a skim of the headlines, a few sentences and it's enough to get the 'gist.' Everybody's an 'expert' these days, yet few actually go deep. Everybody knows three things about a hundred topics, but rarely does anyone know a hundred things about any one topic. Yer tha generation of surface-skimmers, gist-ers and browsers. It's like skipping a rock over the surface of water. Only kids don't skip rocks anymore, they skim through social media posts, blogs and tweets. A flash in the pan, a quick dopamine hit and you're 'updated.' And how much of what these so-called 'experts', 'conspiracy theorists' and 'influencers' or even 'fact-checkers' have been verified? Who's fact-checking the fact-checkers? It's too much, too fast, I say. We all jus' need to take a step back an' catch our breath. The era of the Fast-Timers may well go down in history not as the technological quantum leap that propelled us forward, but as the total collapse of society as we know it." The Pig paused, white space for the student . . .

"Is AI the next industrial revolution that pushes us over the edge? Is AI the Godhead, rendering much of what we now do obsolete? Or will it advance us so far forward in ways which we can't imagine? What if AI falls into the wrong hands? What're we gonna do if A.I., supercomputers, and technocrats start runnin' the show more than they already do? How sustainable is our technological ecosystem? What of the advancing Smart Cities? The Internet of Things? The Metaverse? Are we too reliant on technology? And at what cost? How fragile are our power grids? Our cybersecurity? What of the growing threat of hackers? Are we moving towards a cashless society where all of our financial transactions are tracked and recorded? All of our medical history, commercial activity, social connections—tracked, analyzed and targeted more than they already are? Are we on the brink of technocratic totalitarianism? Our faces, voices and personal information stored in a database somewhere, accessible to who knows how many third parties, government entities or corporations? Is there no such thing as privacy anymore? Are we handing over our constitutional rights in the name of 'convenience?' Unwittingly ushering in the all-seeing eye of Big Brother—the dystopian World State of a Brave New World? Too much and too damn fast . . ." The Pig fell silent.

"I'll tell ya," the Pig cleared his throat again, "We ain't got no time for Fast Time."
The phrase played in Arian's mind.

"Fast Time?" Arian said.

"Fast Time," the Pig said. The way he said it now sounded like a scientific term, like Space Time or Planck Time.

"Fast Time as opposed to what, Slow Time?" Arian said with a bite of sarcasm. The Pig stared back, expressionless.

"Slow Time, like the fairly recent boom in Yoga, meditation and Mindfulness classes?" Arian added.

"God is gonna slow us down, make us humble and teach all these Fast-Timers a long-overdue lesson." The Pig stole back the show.

"Blessed are the meek, for they shall inherit the earth." The Pig swiped saliva from his sausage lips. The swipe came just after he said 'meek', almost as if he ate the words . . . or the meek.

"You see, it is by being humble before God that we shall proceed. Not by going faster, not outpacing the rhythm of God's plan, God's will on Earth. We must remain meek, humble, and submissive."

Are you any of those things, you fucking monster? Arian thought. *Does being your captive qualify as 'submissive?' No, I'm not submissive, nor meek. I won't submit, no. Not until death takes me. Not until I gouge-out your fucking eyeballs. Am I supposed to be humble and feel grateful for this? Grateful that I'm sustained by bread and water? Oh wait, by the occasional piece of steak too? Grateful to be a patron of such brilliant ground-breaking lectures? A perfect little apostle in training? I can see the*

⌁

Lady Gaga pumped into Kirsten's living room from the speakers above her TV. Kirsten bobbed her head to the pumping bass while running in place, mimicking the female trainer on the screen. 'Quaran-train' flashed in big letters across the screen. Live-feed Quarantine workout programs were popular during the Stay-at-Home, self-quarantine. For Kirsten, it was an opportunity to ground into her body and escape the constant 'what ifs'—her missing fiancé, the increased number of RABID-30 infections and the impending global economic collapse experts predicted would follow. She didn't have much free time, but when the hospital occasionally forced her to take a "rest day," she had to occupy her time . . . and distract her mind.

Dark bags showed beneath her eyes, just like they had for many of her overworked and sleep-deprived co-workers. She was alternately under and overeating. And when she did eat, she ate poorly. She didn't have time to cook, so home delivery became the go-to option, being one of the "essential services" allowed. Food too became an escape. Phone calls with her mom and best friend Angela, and Arian's parents as well, became increasingly less effective distractions. As much as her mother was her best friend and greatest confidant, the 'what ifs' remained.

She was having trouble sleeping despite her fatigue and long shifts. She would lay in bed for long periods thinking about Arian. She searched Google Earth and combed over the Mojave, zeroing in on the coordinates of his missing cell phone. She imagined him somewhere out there, like a single grain of sand, crying out to be seen—a desert orphan, an estranged child, calling on a deaf world. Yet a distant hope persisted, calling from the precipice at the end of the earth. She had to know and had to believe—there was no other option—that he was still alive. She also sensed that he wasn't safe and, when she was feeling particularly down, the 'what ifs' attempted to undermine any confidence she had in finding him. The rollercoaster was a serrated blade, cutting away at her emotional stability with every rise and fall.

Some nights she would pace the kitchen floor in the semidarkness, her restless mind like a beating drum. A bathrobe snug around her body and her arms folded across her chest, reminding her of the way Arian used to wrap his arms around her. He gave the best hugs.

The kitchen is where Kirsten felt the most comfortable. It reminded her of her home growing up. Her mom spent a lot of time in the kitchen, cooking up something magical and in the winter, their large, old style oven heated their home like a hearth.

Many important conversations took place in the kitchen. There, she felt she could talk to her mom about anything. Of course, things weren't always peachy, but fights never happened in the kitchen. It was a haven. Food was a form of universal diplomacy, an instant armistice: you set your differences aside, sat at the table and enjoyed one of the world's greatest gifts.

The really serious talks took place in the garage. That's where her parents discussed the big issues, largely out of earshot. Being an only child, Kirsten didn't have a sibling to confide in, so her mom was the funnel, the filter she could pour herself into. Whether she came out feeling cleansed, redeemed or feeling ashamed, her mom was there with open arms and unconditional love. This allowed Kirsten to navigate her 'rebellious' teen phase relatively unscathed.

When Kirsten lost her virginity too young and to the wrong guy, or when she got caught stealing at a shopping mall and had to do community service, her mom was there.

Kirsten came to understand that setbacks and mistakes were part of the grand human theater and were meant to be treated with dignity and compassion. She wanted to create a "kitchen," a safe space for others and thought about being a youth counselor, but ultimately became a nurse.

Now, with Arian missing, Kirsten didn't want to think much about anything. Her goal was to silence thought and disappear into a physical exodus, to lose herself in the pulsing, punishing burn.

"Out of mind," Kirsten said, doing a set of squats. The bass pumped in sync with her movement and sweat streamed down her face. Tears fell from the corner of her eyes, racing down her face along with her sweat. "Out!" She wiped the tears away.

The on-screen trainer said, "Last round girls, let's get those heart rates up!" Kirsten looked at the pulse-rate on her sports watch.

"C'mon!" the trainer commanded. "Push it now; Let's go!! Kirsten followed along, squatting intensely. A lion-like ferocity came over her, burning through the set.

"That's it, that's it!" The trainer's voice was high-pitched but firm. Kirsten squatted down, in sync with the trainer and bass.

"Push it! Push it! Last ten, let's go!!"

Kirsten dropped into a squat, then exploded back up, shaking her mental world.

"Out!" Kirsten commanded, dropping back down into a powerful squat, exploding up to dispel waking demons.

"Five!" Kirsten refused to fall behind as her legs shook beneath her. She pushed on, mimicking the trainer's rhythm and movement.

"You've got this girls!"

"Four!" The trainer roared.

"Get out, out of my—mind!" Kirsten dropped down, her thighs pleading for her to stop, burning as if she were standing in a fire pit.

"That's it girls! Three!"

Kirsten willed her body down into a squat.

"Two!"

"Out!!" She exploded up, thighs and butt burning like never before.

"One!"

"Get OUT!!" Kirsten dropped down, then exploded up for the final time. A thin layer of sweat washed down her body, glistening over her face and arms.

"That's it!" the trainer said.

Kirsten dropped to her butt and fell back, her arms out to her sides like a starfish, gasping for air.

"Good job!" the trainer said. Her voice resounded throughout the room. Kirsten stared up at the ceiling, taking air deep into her lungs.

"Out" she said triumphantly. She closed her eyes, surrendering to the darkness, seduced into the void of no thought. The immediate and primal need of the body was to recuperate; the black, empty void was punctuated by heaping breaths and burning fatigue. As her lungs strained for oxygen, her pores overflowed with sweat; her legs twitched and spasmed, she experienced a sense of peace—the cradle, the womb, the protective primordial ooze. She found her kitchen.

"Hawk calling," Kirsten's smartphone said in a digital monotone, drawing her sleeping consciousness to the here and now.

"Hawk calling," her phone repeated.

I must have fallen asleep, she thought, opening her eyes.

Kirsten sat up and exhaled, expelling the universe. She stood up on two shaky legs and grabbed a towel from the back of the dining room chair and ran it over her forehead.

"Hawk Calling."

She reached for her phone on the kitchen counter.

"Hawk," she said.

"Kirsten, hi," Hawk cleared his throat. "How're you doing?"

"I'm fine. Just finished a workout. What's up?" she said.

"I have some news."

"What is it?"

"Maybe you should sit down," Hawk said calmly.

"Hawk, just tell me—,"

"Kirsten, please . . ." Hawk said.

"Okay, okay." Kirsten took a seat at the dining room table. "Did—did you find him???"

"No, I didn't find him, no . . ."

"Then what . . .?"

"Well . . ." There was silence across the line.

"Hawk, what is it?"

"I found his truck."

"This thing didn't burn up, it was set on fire," Officer Snapp said, circling around the cabin of the truck, as two other officers took photos of the scene. They were all wearing medical masks and doing their best to keep a safe distance apart from one another.

"That's right," Hawk said, following Officer Snapp to the front of the truck.

What remained of the cabin was a charred metal frame, the freight compartment a mere steel skeleton standing idle in the windless desert. The front end was smashed up against a cluster of large rocks. The hood was crushed, the bumper a heap of twisted, burnt metal. Engine parts lay scattered across the sand. The eight-ton chassis sat on six scorched rims, the tires melted into the desert floor like something out of a Dali painting.

Officer Snapp said, "Judging by the burn trail, gas was poured on the top of the hood, splashed up against the freight compartment and inside the cab." He was in his early fifties, had thin silver hair, suspicious, discerning eyes and young energy. He moved around the truck with a spry step, as if his work energized him. The other two officers continued to circle the truck and take pictures. One of them stopped and began sketching a diagram of the scene.

"This thing probably burnt up in less than an hour," Officer Snapp said, throwing a glance at Hawk.

"While most arsonists lack the sophistication to know how to properly disguise a burn as an accident, it's hard to tell if they tried to stop the burn after it got going."

"Tried to make it look like an accident, that's for sure," Hawk said, noting the rock-damaged front end.

"Your missing person, you mean?" Snapp asked.

"No, not him."

"Was he much of a drinker?" Snapp noted an empty whiskey bottle laying in the sand near the driver side door.

"Naw, he wasn't no drunk," Hawk said.

"Under a lot of stress?"

"Who isn't?" Hawk said.

"Right . . ."

"Looks like the license plates were removed," Hawk said.

"That, or they're lying in the scatter somewhere," Snapp said. He walked over and looked between the rock and front bumper where the license plate would have been.

"Either way, looks suspicious to me," Hawk said, peering in through the windows of the cab.

"No sign of a body either," Hawk said, looking through the scatter of burnt debris laying across the floorboards of the cab.

"Nope," Snapp said.

"Doesn't rule out a robbery or kidnapping," Hawk circled round.

"Or murder," Snapp offered.

"Naw, I don't think so. They would have burnt him up along with the truck, or shot him dead," Hawk said.

"Maybe they took him out into the desert and shot him," Officer Snapp tapped his cheek with his pointer finger.

"Murder wasn't the motive," Hawk said.

Snapp took a few steps back and swept his eyes over the desert like a captain looking out to sea on a postcard or in a magazine.

"You say he had no known enemies? Gambling debts, vengeful ex-wives?"

"No." Hawk said.

"Luckily you found the damn thing. It's hidden away in this little outcropping pretty good. No way you'd see it from the Interstate. This must be one of them ol' rancher's roads." Snapp ran his eyes along the path of the road back towards the Interstate.

"What'd you say it's been, a few weeks since he's been missing?"

"That's right," Hawk said, stepping behind the truck.

"We've seen some wild stuff these past few weeks. Everything from fist fights in grocery stores, raiding of food warehouses to the looting of farms for livestock. And with the food shortage scare going around in the media, and the recent hike in food prices, it wouldn't surprise me if someone did steal the truck's supplies. This pandemic has really brought out some crazies."

"Look at this," Hawk was behind the truck, looking down at the sand. The officers walked over.

"I'll be damned. Another set of tire tracks," Snapp said.

Hawk followed along the path of the tires, limping along. The officers followed. The tracks were fairly consistent in the sand and showed deeply where they turned sharply round a bend of large rock, then crawled up a slight incline that headed back towards the Interstate.

"These are deep. Could be a van or pickup truck," Officer Snapp said, his nose on the trail like a bloodhound.

"A pickup truck?" Hawk said.

"Um-huh, could be. The back tires are set deeper into the sand than the front tires."

"Loaded down . . . with groceries? And the weight of 2-3 people?" Hawk knelt down and looked at the depth of the track. The others gathered around him.

"Yeah, could . . . be . . . " Officer Snapp spoke, while tapping his cheek with his finger again. "Could be indeed."

❧

"Sit," the Reptile said, leading Arian, who was blindfolded, to the table.

No dishes?

They sat in silence for some time. The silence finally broke with the sound of the Pig's voice:

"We thank you Lord,

For you are our Shepard,

Guide us out of the Valley of Darkness,

It is Your Name We Honor,

And Your Hand wc Follow,

Out of the Valley of Darkness,

Out!"

Just as the Pig said the word 'Out', the Reptile stripped off Arian's blindfold from behind. Arian opened his eyes to see the Pig seated at the head of the table, assuming his Kingly pose.

"Amen," the Pig said.

The Reptile slithered over and took his seat. The exposed bulb hanging over the table spread a burning yellow light over them. Sensing the Pig's eyes on him, he scrambled to reinforce his mental fortress like a suspect entering an interrogation room. He eyed the stale bread, the hard-boiled egg, and brown beans in front of him. There was also a banana on the table beside his plate. The Pig and Reptile had thick slices of Chicken breast and a side of potatoes. Arian pretended not to notice. He noted the embroidered cross from before, hanging on the wall behind the Pig. He also noticed a calendar nailed to the wall below the cross.

79

That wasn't there before . . . it couldn't have been. He squinted past the light, noting the days of the month crossed off with an X. *Is it really May 10th? Have I only been here for a month?*

He felt the Pig's eyes intensify over him, and he pulled his attention away from the calendar. He shot a glance at the shotgun, which sat in its usual place, across the table, within the Pig's reach, barrel pointed at Arian. There was a radio at the edge of the table, halfway between himself and the Pig. The radio was from decades past, at least a generation older than Arian. It had dust nested in between all its little corners and indentations, like colonies of insects. But it was solid, the kind that would keep on ticking. It clearly showed now as the centerpiece, the new player in the game, commanding the board. The Pig reached over and flipped it on:

" . . . Conservative Extreme-Right protesters are storming the steps of capitol buildings across the country, especially in the South and Midwest. They claim the official Stay-At-Home orders are a violation of their constitutional rights. Tens of thousands held their third day of protests this afternoon in a growing number of states including Ohio, Illinois, and Washington DC in a bid to lift the quarantine and get the economy moving again. Despite the death toll continuing to rise, opposition groups are urging the WHO and state and federal officials to protect the most vulnerable, but allow low-risk individuals to go back to work while maintaining proper safety protocols. The President is expected to hold a press conference later this afternoon."

The Pig reached over and changed the station, settling on a station with a pipe organ accompanying a soft hymn.

The traditional Christian hymn breaks the mania of the RABID-30 update, but therein lies another extreme; one madness replaced by another . . . Madness, Arian thought. The Pig glanced at him and lay his meaty palm face-down, fingertips pointing towards the radio. Arian recognized the hymn, but couldn't quite place it.

"Eat" the Reptile said.

Arian went for the bread while the Pig smacked his lips, slobber hanging from the corners of his mouth. Suddenly the hymn came: *"Ode to Joy','" that's it, that's the one. 'Ode to Joy' . . . Arian thought. 'Ode to joy' that I didn't have to do any dishes before the meal? 'Ode to joy' that I have the privilege to eat at the table again? No chicken for me, but beans?* He started with the bread as always, then the eggs and kept the beans as dessert. The beans were exotic, the "steak" of the meal. But that was where he had made a vital mistake. He has to appear grateful yet at least somewhat indifferent to his 'privileges.'

The Pig's eyes float over, all-seeing, like the Eye of Horus. The hymn . . . Again with the Christian themes? The ACT continues, the curtain is drawn and a pattern emerges—the audience is becoming familiar with the cast of characters. The Master of Puppets is spelling it out—revealing bits and pieces of the script. The dinner prayers, the cross on the wall, the long diatribes rife with End Time premonitions and Luddite philosophy . . . and now 'Ode to Joy'?' Arian thought.

"What's your name?" The Pig asked.

The question came like a jab to the face. Arian blinked and swallowed hard. He considered lying, then said finally; "Arian."

"Aryan?" The Pig said skeptically. "Like the Aryan race?"

"No, of course not," Arian said as if dispelling a lifetime of confusion. "It has nothing to do with the Aryan Race."

"Well . . ?"

"It's spelled differently, for one thing," Arian said.

"What does it mean?" The Pig said with a look of genuine interest.

"It has Welsch origins. It means Silver."

"Silver, as in Gold, Silver, and Bronze?"

"Yes , silver." . . .

"Silver, as in . . . second place?" The Pig said, smirking.

" . . . yeah," Arian dropped his eyes to his plate.

"I see," the Pig said, noting the flash of dejection across Arian's face. The Pig cut into his chicken, the cutting motion drew out time between them. Arian felt the urge to respond, to play along, to participate in the courteous ACT.

"And how about you, what's your name?"

The Pig chewed intently, taking his time, as if considering the question carefully.

"Gipp," he said with a swallow.

"Gipp?"

"That's right." The Pig nodded towards the Reptile, and drawing out the syllables he said: "This here is Ti-le-per."

"Tileper?"

"That's right."

Arian nodded, managing a farcical but well-played half-smile, the best 'nice to meet you' he could muster.

'Gipp,' Arian thought, chewing. 'Tileper' . . . The last time at the table, the Pig didn't ask my name at all. He just went for the throat and asked me if I was married . . . Now he wants to be on a name-to-name basis? He pushed a button last time, now he starts civilly by asking my name? Keep 'em guessin' I suppose. Yeah, let's take it slow now that we've established you are in control of all things, King Pig. Ah, the Puppet Master has grown quite predictable in his ways.

Don't say that! Auggie jumped in. *That's what they want you to think. They create a pattern, lead you by the hand step-by-step, get you accustomed to it and then switch everything on you! You don't dare become complacent now. You gotta keep your guard up at all times. We still don't have a clear motive here. The hardest crimes to solve are the ones that don't make sense. He's establishing a pattern, yes, glad you picked up on that, you privileged little choir boy—ha ha that's funny. Maybe he is grooming you for the choir with all that church music. What's next, you think he'll—*

"Well," The Pig's voice boomed over the table as he lowered the volume on the radio. "You see, we all have 'Names,'" he said. "Names, which are just another form of 'Labeling'."

Arian looked on attentively—a student with a notepad and pen.

"We all have Social Security Numbers, ID cards, licenses, job descriptions, name badges, political affiliations, religions. Age, sex, race, White/Caucasion, Black/African-American, Latin, Asian. . . . These are all labels. Don't forget social and economic status. . . . Who knows, maybe we'll all have barcodes and microchips someday. Maybe that'd be a better way of keeping track of us? All ya need to know about a person can be found right there in that lil barcode. Whether they paid their rent on time, if they ran a red light, how well they did in college. Ya know, a nice little Social Credit Score to keep us all in line? What's next, we report our neighbors for the slightest of infractions? Teach 'em a lesson for cutting in line at the supermarket?"

Sounds like an episode of Black Mirror.

"They've done a pretty good job of defining us and pitting us against each other. They've given us the vocabulary to go around fitting each other in neat little boxes. Ya traitor! Conspiracy theorist! Terrorist! Fascist! Communist! Machista! Homophobe!" If we label each other, define each other, we take sides, cast stones, carve out our differences. Differences that further divide us, weaken us. Classism . . . Class-war . . . Social engineering . . . seems all a bit too convenient, doesn't it? Oh wait, I sound like a conspiracy theorist now, don't I? But we mustn't forget what we have in common, we are all people of this earth. We're all children of God."

The Pig took a breath, as if fuel. He licked his lips and went on: "Divide and conquer is an age-old technique. Very Machiavellian. Used by Julius Caesar and Napoleon. Let the little people fight among themselves, kill each other off, do the dirty work of the oppressors. Then they'll step in and deal with the meager remains."

Arian chewed slowly, his thoughts churning; *Is his diatribe meant to foster a sense of humanity, establish common ground between us? or is it a further mindfuck?*

"Just imagine what we could do if we stopped fighting each other and came together?" The Pig raised an eyebrow. "In a globalized world, wouldn't it make more sense to unite, not divide?"

The Pig sure can shift his tone between a conservative Christian redneck to a luddite philosopher . . .

Now YOU'RE labeling, stop it! He's got you right where he wants you! Auggie barged into Arian's head.

"You have to ask yourself, how much of this is real? How much is social engineering?" The Pig's words once again crowded Auggie out. "How much of this is by the hand of God, or by the hand of the Devil? Revelation 13: 17-18, 'The mark of the beast,' you see, the Number 666--'"

Suddenly a hoarse, dry cough cut in, severing the Pig's string of words. His sausage lips hung in mid-sentence, his eyes darted back and forth, fingers fumbling at the podium. Another sudden, explosive cough hit like a snare drum.

The cough came from down the hall—to the right of where the Reptile is sitting, Arian thought. That hall was separate from the one that led to the hatch and basement. It was long, narrow and dark. The Pig reached over and cranked up the volume on the radio.

The Reptile shot over, took Arian by the arm and rushed him back towards the basement. The last thing Arian heard before he was rushed down the ladder, was the hurried footfalls of the Pig heading in the direction of the cough and the sound of a door slamming shut behind him.

Hawk was reclined in his car, legs spread beneath the dash, his eyes heavy. The clock on the dashboard read 12:48 am. All was dark except for the red digits of the clock on the dashboard, holding the last of his attention like a waning fire. He was parked between Camp A1 and Camp A2, not far from where Arian's truck was found. He nestled the car just off the interstate in the unfenced desert, behind a rocky outcrop of foxtail. The headlights were off, the car's front bumper perpendicular to I-15. He lost himself in the countless hours of observing, but came to know very well, the spare, solemn movements of a still world.

He'd seen ravens scavenging about for carrion and the turkey vultures too, their bald red heads showing at great distances. He'd heard the guttural calls of hawks and the hooting of great-horned owls amidst the Joshua trees. He learned to listen, alright. But mostly he listened to the silence. It often spoke of matters of most importance. Sound was often a distraction from the truth. Movement was a flashy artifice of the physical plane, but silence and stillness were rightful heirs to the land's majesty and its sacred, merciless law.

Aside from the rare delivery truck or highway patrol, very few vehicles passed, and when they did, they came ripping through the void. He spent hours day and night driving up and down the interstate between the two Camps. Between drives, he'd pull over and walk along the road, marking his territory with his boots. His boots kicked up thin bursts of dust and his soles left behind shallow impressions—calling on the desert spirits, announcing his trek into the land. Physical contact with the earth brought him closer to the desert's story, enriching its folklore and calling the mythos to life.

Most of his life he has been searching and following a subconscious urge to bring an image, a face to the story, a cover to the book. Everywhere he went, every case he ever worked on, regardless of the official duty at hand, he was chasing a mythos of his own. According to his native people, the early hours of morning, between 1 and 3 am, is when the veil between worlds is thinnest. This is when the hunt in the shadows begins. The clock read 1:01 am.

Hawk bat his eyes against the drowsiness. His eyelids fell and he popped them back open. They fell again and, in their fall, he caught a glimpse of a black silhouette racing across the interstate. Hawk's eyes widened, only to see an empty stretch of asphalt barely visible in the dark. There was nothing. Nothing but a sleeping world beneath a domed sky; asleep and cooling like an oven recently turned off. He traced the path of the silhouette over the interstate, his mind setting terms to an imaginary contract. Drowsily, he recalled a legend alive in the folklore of his native people—the legend of The Fleeting Shadow, one who is forever hunted but never caught. Many have tested their skill across the desert plains, but the Fleeting Shadow continues to elude all who seek it. However, the sight of the Fleeting Shadow is an omen that one is close to what they seek. It can represent many things, but only the one who lays eyes on it will know its meaning.

Hawk's eyelids fell again and this time he succumbed, closing out one darkness for another, leaving the soft red glare of the clock and the long empty stretch of interstate beyond. The interstate was as still and calm, like a black river.

❧

A cough, it was clearly a cough, Arian thought, hanging from the chains.

A cough—are you sure? Auggie, who lived for conspiracy, was now the voice of reason.

Yes. I heard it twice. The first time I was pretty sure it was a cough, but when I heard it the second time, I was sure.

Positive?

What else could it be?

Where did it come from?

It sounded like it came from down the other hall.

So there could be another person in the house, Auggie deduced.

Arian imagined Auggie's crazy hair, his glasses, the whiskery stubble on his cheeks and chin, his face illuminated by the glow of his laptop, his fingers at the keyboard typing away and pulling up 'evidence' of his most recent conspiratorial obsession.

I'm telling you, I heard a cough. The Pig turned up the radio and the Reptile rushed me out immediately.

But a cough as in choking on food, or a cough as in . . . sick? The word lingered in the darkness.

Sick, of course. It wasn't a choking cough.

So you're saying there is a sick person in the house?

Yeah, I guess so.

Sick with. . . the virus?

Jesus . . . I hadn't thought about that, Arian shrugged.

Or was it all part of the ACT?

I heard a cough, Arian insisted.

Either that, or you've gone completely nuts, Auggie chuckled.

C'mon.

How's it feel to be called the crazy one?

Cut it already!

Listen, you've been down here for what, five, six weeks? Auggie's voice took on a serious tone.

According to the calendar on the wall, about a month, Arian furrowed his brow.

Just a month? Naw, that can't be right, Auggie shook his head.

I didn't think so either, but the calendar said it was the 10th of May.

Really? It just doesn't seem right.

You're telling me?

Doesn't the virus have a fourteen-day incubation period?

That's what they say.

So theoretically, even if you had been infected, you'd be negative at this point. Auggie picked at his stubble.

Theoretically, Arian thought.

So maybe that's why they've been letting you upstairs lately. You're no longer a health risk.

Could be, Arian thought.

Or, since mental deterioration can be a sign of the virus, you already got it and are halfway to the half-way house, Auggie chuckled. *Get it?*

C'mon.

Where's your sense of humor? Isn't your world dark enough?

Damn it, Auggie.

Hey, you know what they say, those who think they're crazy aren't, and those who don't think they are, ARE, Auggie reasoned.

You're a real help. Arian pushed Auggie out of his mind with an exhale. *Insanity isn't an option,* he thought. *They will have to kill me first.*

Suddenly the hatch opened—its long creak, an opening between worlds, a Pandora's Box, a beast's large, gaping maw. The Reptile slithered down, sprayed Arian with antiseptic, then undid both his wrists. He grabbed Arian by the arm and led him up the ladder.

Must be dinner time, Arian thought, the blindfold and duct tape still in place. The Reptile led Arian past the kitchen, and opened the front door of the house. Arian heard a second pair of footsteps emerge from the silence and follow from behind as he was led out the door.

The Pig?

Arian stepped out, feeling the open air on his face. The sun warmed over his body, awakening his skin, rejuvenating his spirit. Just then a blunt object struck him from behind, immense pain shot down his skull to the base of his spine, and he fell face down onto the ground, condemned, once again, to darkness.

❧

Arian woke up and found himself lying on his side, arms tied behind his back and his ankles bound tight as a python. He felt a throbbing pain in the back of his head. An amalgam of rusted metal, dust and mucus choked his nostrils. Light filtering in through his blindfold brought a brighter world, but the heat was suffocating. It thinned the air around him, making him imagine the sensation of being packed in a sardine can.

Am I in the back of a pickup, under a camper top? There was the muffled roar of wind overhead and he could feel the truck bed vibrating beneath him, rolling over the interstate much smoother than he expected.

He was betrayed by a subconscious urge to reach for his non-existent phone. *Shit.* The thought of screaming for help crossed his mind, but his mouth was taped and then came the realization that no one would hear him anyway. Being out of that dungeon, and with the sense of going—the wheels turning below and the sound of air passing overhead—hinted of freedom.

He scraped the blindfold against the truck bed with the side of his head, slowly inching it up his forehead, freeing one eye. He pried open his lashes, wet and heavy with mucus, like a cobweb. Seeing out of one, red watery eye, his vision was blurred by a white halo. He found himself facing the tailgate, indeed lying in the bed of a pickup with a camper shell over top.

The cab and driver must be at my back, he thought. *The Reptile at the wheel and the Pig riding passenger? Will I be disposed of, now that I heard the cough? Could it have exposed a hole in their plan? Will I be taken out into the middle of the desert and shot? Left for the turkey vultures to pick away at my carcass? If it is death, let it come. Let it come, but let me have my fight.*

The pickup slowed, pulled onto the shoulder and sat idling. The driver's side door opened and hung open for a moment before being pulled shut. The pickup began to move again, crawling over windswept dust and pebbly desert rock. The pickup stopped again, the driver's-side door popped open and, a moment later, slammed shut again.

We must've just entered through a gate, Arian thought. *The driver is getting out of the truck to open the gate himself. The Reptile is alone.*

The pickup crawled forward over the hard red sand. They drove on for some time, until finally coming to a stop. The driver killed the engine; his side door popped open again and the tailgate dropped down with a heavy clang. The driver stuck his long, hanging face into the pickup bed as he lifted the latch. Arian pretended to wake up at that precise moment, blinking rapidly and moaning. *It was the Reptile, alright.* The Reptile reached over with his scaly hand, grabbed Arian by the ankle and pulled him across the bed of the truck.

The Reptile sat him up on the tailgate and pulled the blindfold down so it hung under his chin. He undid Arian's ankles but kept his arms tied behind his back.

"C'mon," The Reptile said, nudging Arian with the shotgun barrel. Arian slid off the tailgate and stood on weary legs. The Reptile led him towards an old ranch house. It had a broad porch and closed veranda with drooping eaves. Its shingles were sun-beat; its wooden frame looked as if a strong wind could topple it.

The property was lined by fencing. Beyond, the hazy desert plain stretched far and wide. Arian could also make out an old silo and a water tower, obscured by the halo of his watery eyes, and the dotting of desert shrubs and Joshua trees. The property had a ghostly aura and was likely much more massive than he could tell. As he was led closer to the ranch house, a raven cawed from the distance. Just as they reached the front porch they took a right and followed along a metal fence that ran for quite a distance.

Why did he remove my blindfold? Does he want me to see the ranch? Why did they knock me unconscious, only to let me see this? And why didn't the Pig come along? Though it hurt to think, Arian let go of the questions and realized that, above all else, he needed water.

They reached a metal gate that was cut into the fence. The Reptile held the shotgun over Arian. "Stand aside," he said with a callous, no-nonsense glare. Arian stepped back.

The Reptile dropped the shotgun, hanging from his shoulder on a sling. He pulled out a set of keys, undid the padlock, and they stepped through the gate. They passed through a paddock and entered a large barn with an indoor chicken coop.

"Sit." The Reptile led Arian to a wooden crate beside the coop. The barn smelled strongly of chicken feces. Arian could hear clucking beyond the boarded walls of the coop. It was surrounded by chicken wire. The barn's high ceiling and tall wooden plank walls appropriately reduced Arian to a peasant, a farmhand—a slave groveling at the feet of his master.

The Reptile leaned forward and gave Arian another callous glare. Arian looked back abjectly, submission in his eyes. He could not fight. He could not resist. He was too weary from the blow and the heat. He had no choice but to go along. He knew that if he tried something brash, the Reptile could easily catch him. Besides, he had no idea if the authorities were looking for him or if his burnt-up truck had been found. If so, was he assumed burnt along with it? Surely Kirsten is doing all she could within her power. She certainly wasn't the type to be easily deterred, but there were too many unknowns, too many 'what ifs.' He didn't have the energy to attempt an escape.

The Reptile unbound Arian's wrists, tossing the rope over the same shoulder that had the shotgun sling.

"Water," Arian said. The Reptile slid over to a water tap sticking up from the ground with a tin pail beneath it. He filled the pail and brought it sloshing over. Arian took it with both hands and gulped the water down. It tasted strongly of minerals and old pipe. He palmed water over his face and the back of his head and discovered a massive lump there. However, the water felt cool and rejuvenating, and brought a sense of calm. The feeling stretched on for a few minutes, a shield against the heat.

The Reptile extended a basket. "Eggs," he said, nodding towards the coop. Arian took the basket, stood on shaky legs and slowly walked over to the coop. He flipped up a simple latch and stepped inside. The smell of feces rose up as a dozen chickens scattered away from his footfalls.

❧

"This isn't a 'Missing Person's' case, this is a murder investigation!" Kirsten barked into the phone.

"My fiancé's truck was set on fire!"

"Ms. Kayble, I assure you, we're doing everything we can."

"Everything you can?"

"Everything within the state's power."

"Within the state's power, eh?"

"We're working closely with the state of Nevada as well, in case, for whatever reason, your fiancé crossed over the border."

"Great, and?"

"On our side, in the meantime, we've requested a search helicopter and we'll do a door to door sweep—"

"Door-to-door sweep in the middle of the desert?"

"We'll sweep all residences within the target area," the officer said.

"That's great, but how many officers do you have on the job, it's hundreds of miles of desert we're talking about!"

"Ms. Kayble . . ." the officer exhaled long and hard. "With the pandemic and a cash-strapped economy, we're about as mobilized as we can possibly be." The officer's tone sank to a palpable reality.

"Great, that's just great. Glad to hear you're doing everything within your 'power,'" Kirsten said. "Well, have a good day, officer . . . ?"

"Dalton, Eric Dalton."

"Have a good day Officer Dalton," Kirsten hung up.

"The police are too SLOW. We can only count on them as accessories, back up. We'll get to him first, I promise."

Hawk's words came to Kirsten as she checked the time on her cellphone. Her lunch hour was coming to an end, and soon she would be heading back into the fray.

"SLOW" she repeated the word under her breath as the call to duty weighed on her.

"I don't have time to slow down," she thought, while heading to the decontamination room. She sprayed antiseptic on her hands and scrubbed them thoroughly. Her hands were rough, hardened sheaths. The act of constant cleaning and scrubbing had assumed a neurosis of its own.

"Wish this whole thing could just hurry up and be done with." The thought played over her rigorous scrubbing—scrubbing away of fears, thoughts of Arian, the pandemic, the flailing economy, and the 'what ifs.' She scrubbed and scrubbed, imagining the virus cut down to a microscopic nothingness, a small indiscernible thing washed away with the harsh finality of flowing water, left never to be seen or thought of again as it died the most horrible of deaths, leaving no legacy, no trace, no footprint in the wrinkles of time—dead, gone, taken by the void—flushed down the drain . . . forever.

⌁

"Yes, I understand, Ms. Kayble, we're doing all we can. We'll be in touch," police chief Dalton said, hanging up the phone. He swiveled round in his chair and rubbed the stress lines of his forehead. He sat at his desk, where a mess of files, post-its, and hand scribbled-notes attempted to bury a paper stapler and coffee mug like they were artifacts from an archaeological dig.

"Non-stop, isn't it, chief?" An officer said from a nearby desk.

"Jesus," Dalton said.

"What's it this time?"

"Another missing person's case."

"Missing person? That's nothing these days."

"Sounds more like a suicide too me."

"The nurse's fiancé; is that the one?"

"That's the one. I mean, they're recently engaged, she's working around the clock, and he's been struggling to find work. He finally found work as a delivery driver and boom, the pandemic hit. People are under a lot of stress. They're going crazy—husbands flipping out, leaving their wives . . . wives leaving their husbands. Domestic violence and divorce rates are skyrocketing. People are disappearing into the desert, found hung from Joshua trees or lying in the sand with a bullet hole in their heads. It's terrible. I don't know how many small business owners we've gotten calls about."

The officer turned to Dalton and said: "True. The pandemic is destroying people's livelihood. I mean, me and the wife are struggling, as you know . . . it's affecting us all, really."

The officer was wiry and bug-eyed. He wore thick reading glasses and whistled out his nose when he talked. He had dainty fingers that were thin and pink. He didn't fit the typical police mold. Dalton, on the other hand, fit the classic description— a man thrust into his role by natural ability and talent for wielding authority. He was in his mid-50s, and had years of experience under his belt. However, he was prone to fatigue and, in these trying times, his energy was being pulled in all directions.

Dalton shook his head and said, "I mean, I-15 is a complete Dead Zone. Nothing but desert for miles. Burnt up vehicles and mafia victims tossed to the wasteland. Suicides everywhere. By the time we get to the bodies, they're picked apart by turkey vultures. There's no guarantee we'll find anyone out there."

"Yeah, chances are he just flipped out and took off," the officer said.

"Sadly, I think that's what happened. Poor guy. Poor gal too. She's a nurse, working her tail off. Just not much we can do at the moment," Dalton said thoughtfully. The phone rang.

"Well, back to work," the bug-eyed officer said, slurping down the last of his coffee, springing up from his desk, and rushing for the door. Dalton picked up the phone, fielding his eighteenth call of the day.

Hawk again parked in the desert across the interstate. The cover of oncoming night obscured him into the mix of rock and shrub. His eyes were like a dart zeroing in on a bullseye: a rusted metal gate with an old ranch road that stretched off into the distance, swallowed by the desert's extant void. The outline of vague, distant structures played in his mind. A silo? A water tower? Or Joshua trees, shrub and rock mounds mixed with hopeful delusion? It was the last of the ranch roads and obscure turn-offs between Camps A1 and A2. This one was gated, with an old driveway. It was Arian's last hope, Kirsten's too. But the feeling in Hawk's gut would not be denied; it burned a hole in his belly, a gaping hole that churned like a cauldron of smelting ore. It grew each day that Arian wasn't found. He knew Arian was out there, but his target continued to evade him.

21:37 pm. The digital clock on the dashboard shone red like a candle against the threat of nightfall. Hawk's eyes narrowed over the gate as if honing secret knowledge. He sat watching in the stillness for the rest of the night, having walked up and down the interstate, following along the fence line, monitoring the desert's every move and stealing glances into its playbook. He took slow, deliberate steps over the desert, passing over like a specter in the windless night. His subtle, purposeful movement was like a call and response, a friendly jostling of sorts.

A knock on the door, a peek into a parallel dimension. . . . It wasn't just the contact with dust, sand and rock, not just the warmth of the sun, the cool of the dry desert night, it was the slow sapping of his watery lifeblood that he sought. He had to give something up, to sacrifice his essence, his flesh, his bone. He needed the spirits of the desert to trust him, to rite him into its shared space and reveal its secrets.

The night before, he had parked off the interstate and sat watching the road as usual. When the clock struck 3 am, he built a small fire some yards from his parked car. It was atop a gentle rise in the land, where he could still keep an eye on the interstate. With the land so silent, the slightest movement would draw the world's ear. He took a pinch of tobacco from an old pocket tin, blessed it by raising it to the sky, then held it above the fire. He whispered an offering to the Fire Spirit, then cast it into the tongues of the fire, watching as they swallowed the tobacco in a bright orange blaze. They danced in moving pictures, speaking an ancient language. He knew the language it spoke. He knew too, that relations with the spiritual world weren't built overnight. Omens were earned. He sat at the fire until it died down to ashes, and then ambled off to sleep in the car.

He woke before sunrise and added more rock to the existing stone ring around the fire, fortifying the earthen bond. In the center of the fire pit, now an ashen heap, he built a stone totem stacked twelve high. He laid a hawk's feather at the base. He took a twig and dipped it in the ash, coating its tip. In a tribal tongue, taught by his mother, he sketched out a prayer around the outer ring of the fire. Lastly, he added water from a flask he'd filled some months ago from a head spring on Mount Shasta. He poured it in a spiral, starting at the totem and expanding outwards. He sat crossed-legged, closed his eyes and prayed as the rising sun climbed up over the mountains to the east. He felt the sun's red shadow creep slowly overhead, but didn't open his eyes until it passed completely over, laying claim to the land.

Arian was in the back of the pickup, lying on his side, wrists and ankles bound as before.

Mercy? The Reptile hasn't been violent . . . yet. Aside from splashing water in my face, that is. And the Pig isn't here, of course. Otherwise, I'd probably be knocked unconscious again. The Pig sure likes to threaten with that shotgun of his. Is that his way to show he means business? Keep me guessing, not knowing when or from where the next blow will come?

Arian was exhausted after two days at the ranch—two days in the life of a man's forced betrothal to land. This was his new form of 'dishes.' His bloodied hands, sun-burnt neck, and aching muscles were no consolation prize.

Arian's duties started with gathering hen's eggs and ended with the slaughter of three chickens. The thought brought him back . . . chasing down the chickens, cupping their winged bodies in his hands . . . laying them over a stump, holding their legs still in one hand while raising an ax with the other . . . the chickens squirming and squawking, sticking their necks out straight. The Reptile lorded over him with his vaporous shadow and detached, callous instruction: "Chop, chop!"

Arian's arm shook—the ax high above his shoulder and hesitation weighing his soul. The Reptile barked: "Chop! Chop!"

Hesitation gave way to a forceful, swooping thud—cleanly severing the chickens' heads from their bodies, spitting them dully to the ground. Arian dropped the ax, shuddering as the chickens flopped over and bled out.

Then came plucking . . . a boiling pot of water; stripping feathers from chickens' lifeless bodies; an incision from neck to groin; pulling guts out—fists of squishy, rubbery organs. Arian remembered puking, while the Reptile watched on with shallow, sinister breathing. Arian could still recall the feel of slimy organs in his hands. The chickens were thrown into two large portable ice-filled freezers and thrown into the back of the pickup.

Another flashback slapped him in the face with a punitive hand—a guilt-laden reminder of a karmic act, etched into his record: the image of the vacant open-eyed stare of a dead pig, hanging lifelessly by the hoof, blood spattered against the back wall and along the dusty floor below. Arian wasn't weak-hearted or overly sensitive, but there was something utterly invasive about butchering. The forced, heavy handed slaughter stirred perversely inside him. Arian wasn't a killer; he didn't like doing anything without putting his heart into it. Those forced acts stole a piece of his soul.

And the pointless task of digging a two-foot deep hole into the ground, only to be told to fill it back up again. The midday sun was overhead, the Reptile looking on from a stump in the shade of a tree, a bucket of water at his knee and the shotgun across his lap. Arian dug until exhausted, resting his aching arm over the handle of the shovel, standing knee deep in the hard desert soil. Sweat poured over his body, unremitting, as if from a leaking faucet. He could barely catch his breath between orders to continue. As Arian filled the hole back up again, the Reptile sat watching with that slack-jawed, boyish look of his. When finished, Arian was given water and allowed to sit for a minute. They didn't speak a word. It was as if this fruitless act in the extreme heat held some mystical meaning.

Arian fantasized about plunging the shovel into the Reptile's neck, just below that stupid jaw of his. He imagined **thick black blood** oozing out of the wound, while he twisted the shovel violently—the Reptile reeling back, choking on his dying breaths, gurgling black liquid as it pooled up and spilled over the rim of his mouth like struck oil. Arian shook his head, dispersing the gruesome image. He felt himself being pulled back to the present by an unknown force. After this out-of-body experience, finding his body again felt like a hundred hands from hell pulling him down, down, down.

There he was, back in the present, lying in the bed of the pickup. The blindfold was at a slant across his face, his free eye still blurry. The camper rattled and the bed shook as the truck plunged forth into an endless vacuum of desert air. Nightfall darkened his world once again, trapping him in a tin can, while a faint sheen of moonlight filtered in. He extended his bound hands behind him and felt two large freezers at his back, where the bed of the truck met the cab.

The Reptile can't see me, not with those large freezers blocking his view. He wiggled forward, creating space between himself and the freezers. He pulled his knees as close to his chest as possible, struggling to drop his bound wrists from behind his back, to squeeze under and past his ankles to his front-side. He fought against the tightness of his muscles. The pain was like minions of an evil warlord conspiring against him. He exhaled hard, pulled his knees to his chest again and was finally able to force his wrists past.

Allright, I can use my hands—kind of. It's ok, the Reptile can't see me. Arian repeated this, even knowing that, much like the Pig, the Reptile had an unworldly sixth sense.

He managed to pull his engagement ring from his pocket. He closed his eyes and lay there thumbing it. After some time, the pickup began to slow. As the truck made a turn off the interstate, Arian wiggled his way towards the tailgate. Finally, the truck came to a stop in front of a metal gate. Arian turned the simple latch and slightly raised the camper shell hatch. Trembling, he dropped the ring out of the narrow opening.

Meanwhile, Hawk sat in his car, parked off the interstate in the same place he'd been for the past two nights. His eyes grew heavy over the metal gate guarding the old ranch road. He blinked hard, then flicked open his eyelids, signaling the beginning of an on-going battle with the night. Suddenly a white rusty pickup truck with a camper shell cut into view, rumbling down the interstate, a floating white speck appearing in the dark. He blinked it away, half thinking he imagined it. The floating speck became clearer as it pulled closer into view. He sat up and leaned forward over the steering wheel. He watched the truck slow, then turn off the interstate towards the metal gate he'd been watching. It stopped and sat idling as the driver got out. The driver was abnormally tall and wore a sun hat and overalls. He opened the gate, returned to the truck and drove through—then got out to lock the gate behind him before driving on.

Hawk watched as the truck continued up the road, trying to make out the numbers on the license plate. He reached for a set of binoculars, just as its tail lights disappeared into the distance.

Hawk reclined in his car as the sun burned over the roof like an iron over an ironing board. The heat invaded his dreaming mind, seeping in and by degrees melting away the remnants of dreamscape—a black silhouette standing at the horizon, facing Hawk as he rushed toward it. As intensely as Hawk pursued, the silhouette remained at a fixed distance, as if Hawk were running on a treadmill. The silhouette stood unmoving; baiting in its expressionlessness as the ground between them rolled on endlessly.

Hawk drove his feet against the ground, trying to propel himself forward. He reached out a hand and screamed. His legs ached and grew slow and heavy. He pulled them from the ground as if they were stuck in mud, each step an extraordinary act of will, draining precious breath.

The still figure stared fatedly back.

"NOOOOO!" Hawk screamed, struggling to push on, as his lungs burned with ice. "Nooooooo!" Hawk jerked to consciousness, sweat beading up on his forehead, his heart jumping in his chest.

"Jesus," he said, sitting up. The weight of the dream hung over him as if holding lasting consequences in the waking world.

He reached for a pack of cigarettes in the center console, stuck one between his lips and lit it. He hung his arm out the window and brought his eyes towards the waking sun. He took a drag, feeling the nicotine rush in to quiet his lungs. He exhaled a puff of gray smoke. In the smoke, he saw an image of a silhouette . . . dispersing. Seeing himself struggle to run towards it, he experienced the torturous, laborious sensation of running in place.

Therein lay a responsibility he'd tried to set down many times, a mission he wished to retire. It was an acquiescence—not to an enemy, but to a part of himself that stubbornly continued to pursue the non-pursuable. His father never wanted to be found; if he ever was, it wouldn't go well. A part of Hawk understood this simple reasoning. Another part of him could not be reasoned with . . . After some minutes, he felt the gravity of the dream lift. He flicked the cigarette out of the window and looked towards the metal gate across the interstate.

The sudden memory of the white pickup he had seen the night before—cutting down the interstate, entering through the gate and disappearing up the farm road—came to him now. Hawk glanced at the time on the dashboard. It read 11:43 am.

He threw on his Stetson, flipped the ignition switch and crawled across the desert. He crossed over I-15 to the opposite shoulder and parked fifty meters or so down from the gate. He flipped his emergency flashers and lifted the hood of his car. Walking over to the gate, his eyes drew inward, narrowing beneath the brim of his Stetson. He smelled the air and tilted his ear to the windless sky. He leaned over the gate, eyeing a pair of tire tracks and traced them up the old road as far as he could see.

He nodded, the corners of his mouth tightened, curling his bottom lip into his chin. He traced the tire tracks back to the gate, along the shoulder where the gravel gave way to sand and dust. A sharp reflection cut into the corner of his eye. He turned and laid eyes on a metallic object laying in the gravel to the side of the gate. He stepped over, squatted down and picked it up. It was a silver ring. His heart contracted as a dark energy washed over him and the hair on the back of his neck stood up.

Arian bit into a piece of chicken thigh, tearing it from the bone. The Pig's eyes held clinically over him as if he were a lab rat.

"Nothing like eating food prepared by one's own hand?" The Pig said this more like a statement than a question. Arian stiffened as the Pig's words conjured an image of a beheaded chicken lying on a stump. *Christ*, Arian thought, his finger twitching as he reached for a fork, eyeing the chicken on his plate. *Damn it. The twitching of my fingers, another perceived weakness, show of fear. You can't let him get . . . to you . . .*

"Don't you think?" the Pig added, again as a statement. His words seemed to shrink the table and cause the chicken to grow large on their plates. The Pig, the Reptile, and Arian sat in their usual places at the table, their first meal together since Arian's and the Reptile's return from the ranch. It was like returning from a long exodus from some distant land—exhausted and starved, yet imbued with a strange mystical aura. Arian felt as if he had embarked on a great pilgrimage to Ramadan or the Camino de Santiago. Did the labor pains and suffering he'd experienced at the ranch make him stronger and . . . more appreciative?

There's nothing spiritual in the land of the morally depraved. You're both clearly insane and you'll pay in blood for your deeds. Arian noted a familiar gleam in the Pig's eyes and the beginning of that slowly curling sneer of his. Arian braced for the sermon.

"You see," the Pig cleared his throat with a grunt. "You Fast-Timers grew up with everything in the palm of your hands. Quite literally. The advent of Smart technologies, advanced algorithms and AI automate your everyday lives, your day-to-day experiences. Everything from google search algorithms, navigation apps such as google maps, to self-driving cars. When's the last time you didn't use google maps to get somewhere? You're too reliant, going too fast, there isn't much use for thinking anymore. Thinking is becoming obsolete, replaced by 'accessing' information—running a program or system to do the thinking for you." The Pig said, assuming a scholarly tone.

Haven't we been doing that all along? Creating technology to make our lives easier? There will always be a human tendency to create technology to do the work for us, Arian thought. It wasn't that the Pig didn't say some thought provoking things, but it was his outright contradictions—the promotion of anti-technological ideologies while using a shotgun, radio, and electricity. Given his supposed Christian faith and apparent religious 'purity,' how can he possibly justify robbery, kidnapping, and acts of violence?

There are many forms of madness . . . and some of us seem to be afflicted with more than one form at the same time, Arian thought.

"I bet you miss having your cell phone? Forever at your side, like a faithful servant? When you parted ways with it, did it feel like you lost a part of you? Like a war vet who experiences phantom pains, can you still feel the ITCH?" A glow of condescension floodlighted over the Pig, his spine straightening with the words, his piggish nose tilted slightly up. The Pig went on: "Kids today can barely use a pen, let alone a screwdriver or even . . . an AX."

The word rammed images into Arian's mind: the chickens—bloody, twitching and beheaded. The Pig continued: "You're handed everything on a silver platter," the Pig said, eyeing the plate of chicken in front of Arian. He went on:

"You city slickers never had to put your hand to anything, toil in the fields, break your back beneath the beating sun. Everything is increasingly mass produced, ready-made, convenient, and customized. You are the generation of Short-Minds and Fast-Times. Where does the journey lead, what significance could it possibly have, if it's merely a rushed, five-second spurt, an ejaculation of the mind, body, and so-called 'soul?' The cursory, pre-ejaculation of the Fast-Timer."

"So, you mean our daily lives are increasingly filled with meaninglessness and triviality?" Arian said.

"That's the GIST of it," the Pig said.

"Kind of like digging a hole, only to fill it back up again?" Arian said.

A long, slow sneer spread across the Pig's face.

"You're sick!" Arian jerked forward. Spittle fell from his mouth and dotted the table.

"Funny, I could say the same thing about you," the Pig said.

"YOU'RE calling ME sick?"

"Your entire generation, really" the Pig said, raising an empty hand and pretending to thumb at a cell phone.

"And what about you, huh?" Arian said.

"Well?" The Pig's face flushed a deep red, conjuring iniquities.

"You fuckers aren't human!" Arian said, wiping his mouth as his heart-rate kicked up. The Pig's sneer widened, revealing a canine. Arian tucked his chin, angling his forehead forward like a battering ram. Acts of violence played in his mind. A hint of pride spread over the Pig's face, like from a teacher to a promising student.

The Pig went on: "Is it no surprise that depression and drug use are on the rise? If nothing is earned, everything so easily given, every urge instantly satisfied, what could we possibly be proud of? What could we possibly value in a society? Heck, kids don't even play in backyards anymore. They play computer games and compete for 'likes' on their latest selfie posts. Men are becoming increasingly emasculated. Kids are so damn sensitive, detached yet in need of constant approval. They can't even take a joke. 'Snowflakes' as they say. Yet everyone is tough behind a keyboard. And everyone is so damn 'happy' according to their latest post, living a perfect life in a digital paradise. But strip yourself of your precious online persona, internet avatar and echo chamber of yes-men, and then what? Can you face the real world? The non-virtual YOU? Is having to face the real world, where one cannot escape into fantasy 24/7, becoming the very definition of modern man's 'struggle'? So accustomed to escape and fantasy, you're incapable of dealing with the slightest REAL difficulty? At the word 'difficulty', the Pig leaned back in his seat.

Difficulty? Arian thought. *Who wouldn't go insane after pointlessly digging holes and then burying them back up again? . . . Perhaps we're all pointlessly digging holes . . .*

'YOU Fast-Timers,' 'YOU kids.' Is he belittling me? Is he trying to get personal? Arian bunched his brow. *Well, it's BEEN personal, you sick fuck. 'Snowflakes,' huh? He's calling me soft. Well, maybe I am soft on killing chickens, but there's a certain Pig I wouldn't mind axing.*

For a rancher, he sure seems to know a lot about social media and current social trends . . . yet I haven't seen them use a cell phone, computer, or TV. They don't seem to have anything in the house that was made in the last two decades.

Suddenly he felt the Pig's eyes burning over him, distantly, as if standing away from a fire but still feeling its heat. Arian raised his brow, as if to say 'continue, I'm listening.' But the Pig didn't speak. He simply scooped up a piece of chicken from his plate.

The Reptile picked at his plate in his usual unassuming manner. His shaggy red hair fell over his eyes as he dropped his chin to eat, hanging that long dumb face of his. His dark energy was again at his side, subservient. They sat in silence until all their plates were empty. Finally, the Pig looked across the table at Arian, calling upon his eyes to rise up to meet him.

"You own that ranch?" Arian said boldly. The Pig's face opened up with a curious, childlike playfulness, as if he had long anticipated the question.

"The ranch?"

"Where I was just taken. The chickens. The holes," Arian said, his brow folding, accentuating the battering ram.

"It's in the family," the Pig said, placing a proud fist on his hip. The word 'family' carefully punctuated.

Keep him talking, Arian thought.

"You see, this country was founded by immigrants. My family was no different. They were Irish immigrants of the post-famine era— hard-working farmers making due, living off the fat of the land. My family of farmers goes back four generations. Ol' grandpappy had a knack for knowing where to be at just the right time. He hit a stroke of luck out in the silver mines of Nevada, took his small fortune and invested in land on the California side. Clever man, he was."

"Irish?" Arian said.

"Explains ol' Red here," the Pig motioned at the Reptile's shaggy red hair.

"Ain't got no more hair of my own," the Pig said with a laugh. His laugh was disturbingly self-satisfied and narcissistic. It was the type of laugh that found joy in one-sided self-amusements, like laughing at one's own jokes, or excessive celebration of one's own successes.

So his family owns that ranch, eh? Arian thought. *And this old farmhouse too, I suppose. Old money. But that ranch was deserted, although I'm sure I only saw a fraction of it. How big it really is, is hard to say. I was weary, dehydrated, and overworked. I couldn't concentrate on much, it's true. Is this his way of endearing me into his 'family' of farmers and ranchers?* Arian thought. He swallowed the last bite of chicken and wiped his mouth.

"Nothing like eating food prepared by your own hand," the Pig again eyed Arian's plate, repeating his line from earlier, this time with a peculiar forbearance. At those words, the Reptile stood and slithered over to the kitchen and warmed a pot on the stove. The kitchen became eerily quiet. The Pig kept his gaze steady over Arian but said nothing.

"Sharing what you create is the best gift one can give," the Pig said after some time, as the Reptile returned with a bowl of Chicken soup. Arian looked up as the Reptile stood over him, holding the steaming bowl like a dumb waiter.

"Stand," the Reptile said. Arian stood and the Reptile handed him the bowl. Arian took it and stood there, puzzled. The Reptile led Arian by the arm towards the other hall, the one that the Pig had slipped away into the time before, the one with the source of the mysterious cough—the one that played along the shadowy edges of fear. His heart kicked up. He felt the Pig watching him as if he were a child, pupil, or employee—off on his own after days of training.

The hall's plain shadow-darkened walls seemed to crawl as the Reptile led him through, the ceiling seemingly collapsing down. As they reached the door at the end of the hall, sweat ran down Arian's forehead. His hands trembled, and he sloshed the soup. The Reptile turned the door knob and the latch snapped free. The door opened in slow motion and, as it swung wide, it revealed a dirty white wall with a large partially opened window with a beige curtain and a hardwood floor; then the foot of a queen size bed came into view. As the door continued to swing, the figure of a woman, grotesquely obese with dry, sickly pink skin like the Pig's, came into view. She lay in the bed as if it were an extension of her body. She had dark pebbly eyes, exactly the same as the Pig's. Her thinning gray hair was regal somehow— stubbornly clinging to her head like the dying mane of a lion.

The memory of the choking cough he'd heard some days before came back to Arian now—sounding like a cannon behind his ears. His eyes were fixed on the Woman as a sick, perverse world unfurled before him. He felt like he had stepped into an insane asylum. The room smelled like body odor and rotten apples. The opened window did little to mitigate the stench. The room felt pressurized, like a balloon about to burst. The Reptile led him to the Woman's bedside. The Woman's eyes swung over and pierced him to the core, like a spear. Arian shook and the soup sloshed over the bowl, spotting the hardwood.

The Pig's words repeated in his mind: "Sharing what you create is the best gift one can give."

∽

"Sit, please," Kirsten said.

Hawk took a seat at the dining table, keeping his medical mask on, he took off his Stetson, leaned forward and rested his forearms over the table. Kirsten poured him a glass of water from a carafe.

"Thanks," he said.

She took a seat across from him. She too was wearing a mask, but he noticed thick swabs of makeup attempting to hide the puffiness beneath her eyes. Her reddish-blonde hair was tied back in a ponytail. It was a mess of split ends. She wore a light blouse that hung over her shoulders. Her workout routines and busy work schedule showed in her shoulders, neck and arms like an action figure, an everyday Superwoman. But her eyes were drained of their usual tenacity.

"So tell me, how are things?" Hawk said.

"Uff, where do I start?"

"Anywhere you'd like," Hawk said with a nod.

"The police still aren't doing much, eh?" she said.

"With the pandemic and all, we were lucky to have Officer Snapp out to see the truck," Hawk said.

"Yeah . . . I'm on the phone, nagging them every day, hoping to light a fire under their asses.

"Good," Hawk said.

"It makes me feel better, somehow. Just the hope that they might do something . . . find something, find . . . him. They said they'll do a door-to-door sweep, send out a helicopter and get more highway patrol on the job . . . but yeah, with the pandemic and all . . .

I don't know. I really don't know what's possible," she turned and looked away.

"All we can do is to keep that spark lit under their asses. I have Officer Snapp's personal number. He was able to confirm it was in fact Arian's truck that we found burnt up. He's looking into the other set of tire tracks that were on the scene, too."

"That's good," Kirsten said, perking up.

"I was also able to get Dalton's cell phone number. I think he got tired of me swinging by his office so damn much. I get on his ass pretty good. Something tells me they'll be taking Arian's case a bit more seriously now," Hawk said.

"God I hope so. I've been talking with my mom, and my best friend is calling constantly. Not to mention Arian's parents. They are scared shitless, as you can imagine. 'Are you ok? Have you heard anything?' I just want to say 'yes, everything is fine, everything is fine.'"

In her mind, Kirsten was back in the protective womb of her mother's kitchen. She was in her safe zone where anything large or small was going to be ok. It was where she could face her deepest darkest secrets and fears. To some degree, she felt she could confide in Hawk too.

"How're things at the hospital?" In her eyes Hawk saw her need to talk, the need to let it all out.

"It's a mess. I mean, on the one hand, we've got an amazing team. We work so well together, it's incredible, really. We've got each other's backs. You couldn't ask for a better team at a time like this." She wiped back a tear.

That's it, let it all out, Hawk thought.

She wiped back another tear. The motion was quick and decisive, like a martial arts move. As her face grew hard, Hawk could see strength stemming up from an imperceptible depth. He knew there were many sensitive warriors in this world. Their sensitivity is what made them dangerous. Without knowing peace, how could one know war? Hawk knew that Kirsten was ready to pick up her sword and shield. Having warded off her demons, she emerged with chin high and eyes on the horizon. This was his moment. This was the Kirsten he needed to speak to.

"Listen," Hawk said.

Kirsten turned, looking over as the light filtered a confetti of golden streaks over him.

"Give me your hand," Hawk said, extending his. Kirsten shot him a quizzical look.

"Please," Hawk said. She slowly extended her hand.

He took it and flipped it over so the palm faced up towards the light.

"Relax" he said, watching as the filtered light played over her palm.

"Take a deep breath." She closed her eyes and drew in a long breath. He held her hand at the wrist, feeling her pulse.

"Take another breath," he said. She did so, and he felt the Warrioress in her take root. He felt her blood pulse, her breath flow like a powerful stream between concrete banks, a symbiotic system not AGAINST, but FOR.

"I have something for you," he said. A small, light object touched the center of her palm. She opened her eyes: "Oh my God!"

Hawk let go of her wrist. "His ring!" She raised the ring to the light with her thumb and index finger. The light played over the ring in brilliant golden streaks. Tears raced down her cheeks. She then held the ring beside her own, which was fitted on her finger.

"It's his ring, it's definitely his!" she said.

"I thought so," Hawk said.

"Where did you find it?"

"Off I-15, in front of a gated driveway."

"Gated driveway?"

"One of those old ranch roads, the kind that looks abandoned or seldom used . . . but used," Hawk said.

"Between the two Relocation Camps?"

"That's right. It was within the target area, exactly where we'd expect it to be," Hawk's face opened subtly, as if revealing clues to a well-constructed plot.

"Holy shit, I can't believe it—" Kirsten held the rings side by side like reunited twins.

"You think it was stolen?" Kirsten asked.

"It could have been," Hawk's face said otherwise. "But I have been combing over that exact area day and night," he said.

"So what are you saying?"

"It wasn't there before."

"Before? As in—?"

"It wasn't there a day ago."

"Are you absolutely sure?"

"Positive," Hawk said.

Kirsten's face drained of its color. "So what you're saying—" she held Arian's ring in her hand—as if a part of her was reuniting with him. She wasn't a superstitious person, but at this moment, she could believe anything. She swallowed hard.

"What you're saying is that he's out there, he's . . . alive?" she choked on the final words.

"Yes."

"Yes?" Kirsten said, as if trying to make an abstract concept fit reality.

"He MUST be," Hawk said.

"So let's call the police, get a warrant to search the property, let's—"

"It's not that easy. In the eyes of the law, finding Arian's ring outside a gated ranch road off the interstate in the middle of an endless desert doesn't necessarily prove anything. It certainly puts my hair on edge, but we're probably gonna need more for a warrant. I'll get in touch with my lawyer buddy, Officer Snapp, and Dalton too. See if I can light that fire you're talking about."

"Uff, Dalton. He's not doing shit," Kirsten said.

"With the pandemic and all, the wheels of bureaucracy have nearly ground to a halt. . . but that won't stop me . . . or us. "

Kirsten nodded, and beneath the glow of the lamp, she felt a renewed sense of hope.

"Look, as I said, I know a lawyer. I'll see what he can do. We'll try to get the police involved as best we can, but I think we're mostly on our own for now," Hawk said. Kirsten nodded.

"We can't just go knocking on ranch doors, asking questions. Not yet. We've got to be very careful how we approach this," Hawk added, his voice calm.

"Well, I'm all ears."

"Good, because I have an idea," Hawk said, elbows on the table, enlacing his fingers together, with his chin over his knuckles.

"An idea?"

"Yes." He peered shrewdly across the table. Kirsten's energy calmed and the initial shock left her body, the Warrioress within now firmly rooted.

"Listen closely," Hawk said.

Arian hung from the chains. Pain came in sharp jabs and pulsed along now familiar places. After several hours of standing, he'd switch to kneeling, or vice versa. Each position served specific entrées of torture, each transition an escape from one pain-state to another, each with the sense of falling . . . falling hopelessly back into the cradle. The cradle, then the womb . . . the womb of death. 'Resistance' was a mantra sustaining him from one moment to the next. But it was short of guarantees. His only resistance to this existence as a puppet, a plaything, and an atrophying mannequin was his ability to enter the occasional stillness of non-thought.

The puppet master has his way . . . for now, he thought.

The dark of the basement (further darkened by the blindfold) became familiar again. Back from the bloody slaughtering, pointless hole-digging, and the punishing heat of the ranch, he almost missed the basement's silence, its stillness. It was virtually impossible to tell how long he'd been held captive. He thought he'd been there for an eternity before he'd been taken to work on the ranch. The calendar in the dining room said nearly a month had passed. Was he at the ranch for two days? Three days? The blow to the head didn't help. Migraines continued to drain him of energy, making it hard to think.

He was quite certain he'd been taken up to eat at the dining table with the Pig and Reptile at different times of the day, never consistently for lunch or for dinner— just to confuse him? The food didn't always correspond to a 'lunch' or 'dinner' meal either. And although he'd seemingly gained a bit of vitality from having eaten eggs, steak, and chicken, he'd been hauled off to work on the ranch, drinking only a minimal amount of water, and given no food while there. He expended every ounce of energy a hearty meal could afford. The rollercoaster continued, and even the semblance of a quiet, calm basement could easily be interrupted at any time by the sudden opening of the hatch.

At any moment he could be abducted to a world of servitude, inexhaustible diatribes, and ideological sophistries. Sometimes during a peaceful stretch of contemplation, he'd hear the distinct whine of the hatch and the Reptile slithering down the ladder. Arian's neck and shoulders would tense up, sensing his dark vapory energy approach, only to realize he'd imagined it all.

The blind silence was neither friend nor foe, merely an amalgam of seemingly fixed yet ever-changing circumstances—a plaything of his mind, a plaything of THEIR mind. He was on a string controlled by the puppet master's fingertips. The moment he began to enjoy the peace and quiet, it turned against him—once again at the mercy of his growing insanity . . . or theirs. The darkness, the blind silence . . . he could paint it whatever color he wanted, else it painted itself.

And when the silence grew stale, old devices arose anew; *See, they've successfully conditioned you to recognize 'privileges,'* the voice of Auggie came to him now.

Auggie was smart; he knew he was smart, but his theories took great creative liberty at times.

Isn't it nice to get a break from the butchering of animals and escape the sun-beaten thralls of hard labor? Do you miss the red sun burning over your back? Is that a tan I see? You look a little red, pal.

Arian imagined Auggie's signature smart-ass grin creeping over his face. *As playful as it is, that grin of his deserves a swift slap from time to time,* Arian thought.

You see, you are supposed to feel 'privileged' to be left alone in the dark now, as opposed to breaking your back under the hot sun. It was just as you had felt 'privileged' to be taken out to the ranch, out of this damn basement and get some fresh air. They are conditioning you to appreciate the conditions of your captivity, Auggie said.

Silence stretched out for some time, as if weighing Auggie's point.

I know it's dark in here, but I bet you're as red as a lobster, all sun-burnt and all, ha ha, Auggie chuckled.

Shut up, Arian snapped. All jokes aside, he was happy to have the company of another person—at least abstractly.

Auggie changed his tone: *Listen, what about the Woman? What a trip, eh? Is she the Pig's wife? She has those same devious pig eyes and sickly pink skin. They made you serve her like she was a Queen. What next? You'll be massaging her feet?*

Aw, C'mon.

But really, what about her coughing, eh? Think she has Ravid-30? Lung cancer? General poor overall health? Is that why they raided your truck? The need for over-the-counter medicines, multivitamins, antiseptics and all? All kinds of illnesses, diseases and pre-existing conditions have been put on the back burner as the world prioritizes the Ravid 30; maybe she's seriously ill? Is that why you were quarantined in this basement for weeks before being allowed upstairs, or in the same room as her?

Arian nodded as Auggie's narrative congealed in an intriguing mind soup. The abstraction fit the tangible. The tangible fit the abstract. The madness became more maddening and therefore sane, somehow.

What if she is really sick? You only heard her coughing on that one occasion. Was it just a smoker's cough? She's seriously obese, immobilized, it's true. Her bed was like a wheelchair, like an extension of her physical body. We could say that she is sick in the physical sense, no? But it wasn't clear that she had any flu-like symptoms. If she was sick with the flu or even the virus, would that explain the chicken soup you brought her? Or was it just another act within the theater?

Auggie's words flowed through Arian's mind, stimulating more thought, wheels spinning with no traction; multiple freeways of incoming thought bombarded him all at once.

Oh, and what about the ring? Auggie added yet another lane. *If there is a search crew after you, think they'll find it?*

Yeah, why not? Arian said.

Yeah, surely they will. Auggie said.

Arian needed to hear that. He did not dare think of anything less. *They will surely find it, yes.* He couldn't think of the possibility that the authorities may have already written him off as another pandemic panicker—another desert suicide case. He could not think that perhaps they'd already combed over the vast 'Dead Zone' of the virus-stricken Mojave and come up empty-handed. He could not give up hope that Kirsten was forever determined to find him, that he'd get to see her beautiful hazel eyes again, that he'd be able to wrap his arms around her and feel her body against his.

He shed a tear as the thought of human touch seemed so remote—a fleeting abstraction, a memory on the brink of extinction. Just then the piercing whine of the hatch came from above, raising the hairs on the back of his neck. He sucked up his tears, pushing Kirsten far from his mind. Soft footfalls descended the ladder. The slithery, airy quality of the footfalls soundlessly approached and that familiar vapory energy filled the basement. Arian tensed up as a large hand gripped him at the wrist.

❧

Arian's hands smelled of dishwater. He'd served the Woman the last of the chicken soup, and now sat on a chair facing her across from her bed. The bedroom smelled like body odor and rotten apples, just like before. The window was partly open—the beige curtain blowing in a light breeze. A ceiling fan whirred overhead. Despite the fan, the room felt naturally cool as if this part of the house was nestled beneath the shade of a tree. The Pig sat at the Woman's bedside with his familiar smug, regal demeanor. He leaned back against the chair, one fist on his hip, shotgun across his lap. Despite their presumptuous air, the Pig and the Woman were unspeakably grotesque. This haunted their dynasty like a proud, black secret.

The bowl of chicken soup sat on the Woman's cleavage between her enormous sagging breasts. She wore a thin blouse that stretched against her body, like a plastic bag filled with air. A rose-motif blanket was pulled up to her hips, covering her legs. She spooned soup to her mouth, slurping loudly.

Arian's stomach turned, as the sound of the slurping and the choking mix of body odor and rotten apples attacked his nostrils. He now became aware of his own sweat and odor. He'd been wearing the same clothes since he'd been back from the ranch, where he'd been given coveralls. This added to his overall discomfort yet, at the same time, made him feel more accustomed to his surroundings. The constant heat and sweating, the toil of misery and isolation . . . at times nearly made him feel as insane as his captors. It was like partaking in communal misery—soldiers suffering trench warfare, or prisoners in a chain-gang.

"You've been here for some time now," the Woman said, looking up from her spoon. The soup spilled over her thick lips, which

115

like the Pig's, looked like fat sausages. Her voice sounded almost pleasant. This ran counter to her dry, peeling and sickly skin, those large exaggerated sausage lips, her big upturned nose, and wide, flaring nostrils. Her black, pebbly eyes held a sinister intelligence no pleasant voice could mask. Arian looked back, unsure if a response was warranted.

"You miss your family? Friends?" She asked.

Arian rubbed his finger where his ring used to be. Caught off guard by her directness, he adjusted his back against his seat. He'd half-expected an inexhaustive speech or hell-bent sermon.

"It's ok, I don't bite," she said, slurping.

C'mon, hold a conversation; buy time until someone finds the damn ring! The voice of Auggie barged in.

"I miss everything," Arian said.

"Everything?" The Woman repeated as if it were a philosophical question.

"Well," she said, setting the empty bowl on a bedside table. She wiped her mouth with the back of her hand, cleared her throat and folded her fingers over her belly. She raised her eyebrows, signaling the start of the diatribe he'd been expecting.

My two cents aren't wanted; I'm a pupil here to be indoctrinated, Arian thought.

Just play along, will ya? Auggie said.

"You'll surely be missing some things about the old world. The world simply cannot return to its former state, not after a pandemic of this magnitude. Socially, politically, . . . globally we are gearing up for a great reset. The grand reconstruction. First a pandemic, then worldwide economic collapse is sure to follow. And with the wave of violent protests sweeping the country, we may be on the brink of civil war." Her words marched out stolidly.

"I heard," Arian said.

"Oh yes. Our country is polarized, lines drawn deep into the sand. There are those who feel the quarantine—the Stay at Home Order is a violation of their constitutional rights."

"I see," Arian said.

"Angry mobs are flooding capital buildings and rioting in the streets. Looters, anarchists, and radical, so called anti-fascist groups are wreaking havoc. Nobody knows what's going to happen. These are uncertain times. Historic times of uncertainty. Biblical, even. Reactive, everyone is so reactive. Ahhh, The Fast Times of the Fast-Timers," the Woman said with an exhale.

Fast-Timers, Arian thought. *Where have I heard that?* Again he rubbed his finger, a self-comforting impulse, a nervous habit—not unlike a teenager in school detention or a boring class, checking the clock in hopes that it would end. Or perhaps like the need to check a text, tweet or social media post. A need for distraction? Or was he simply accustomed to constant stimulation? He didn't have the energy to engage in any debates with her now. It was his opinion that every generation is critical of the one before, and is rarely if ever accepting of the changes to come. The human ego grounds one in the superiority of MY time, MY culture and MY views. No one wants to admit that their world is outdated—their ideas, tastes and fashion no longer take center stage, the rhythm of their step is outmoded.

Despite the 'call and response' format the Woman was seemingly inviting him to participate in, he knew he was there to listen.

"So when you say you miss 'everything,' I imagine that it means family, friends, a girlfriend, or wife . . . a pet, perhaps," she said, sounding thoughtful.

"Yes," Arian said.

"Family is our world's most precious resource. Our most valuable treasure. With every passing decade, a wedge is driven deeper into the family structure, forcing it apart. There was a time when a single family income was enough to support a family, but nowadays a dual-family income isn't enough. Both parents work full-time and the child is thrown into daycare. 'Family values' they say. What value is being given to families when the vast majority cannot afford to have a family? Not to mention adequate maternity leave, vacation time or medical care." She cleared her throat again, repressing a cough.

Talking takes effort. She doesn't necessarily enjoy it. The Pig could lecture to a crowd of thousands for hours on end, basking in the sound of his own voice, whereas talking seems to exhaust her. Perhaps it's her 'sickness?' There is a clear energetic difference between the Pig and the Woman, although they are both clearly sick, but in discernibly different ways, Arian thought.

"Sick," the Woman said.

Right on cue. Arian furrowed his brow. A smirk spread across the Pig's face, taking in every subtlety, every nuance of Arian's reaction—stolen away and sealed in a vault deep within the Pig's dark world.

"This generation suffers from a neurosis of 'ME.' You are going too fast, outpacing your own attention span, outstripping your own cognitive abilities. More, more, more . . . faster, faster, faster. A self-indulgent self-suicide of sorts. The world is experiencing an absolute decline in values, traditions, and meaning." The Woman paused and raised a finger to scratch at a flakey patch of skin on her cheek.

She's echoing what the Pig was saying. Is this her way to see if the student is paying attention? What, will there be a quiz on this stuff later?

"Sick," the Woman said again.

Although we live in stressful, rapidly-developing times—and it's quite possible there will be some drastic changes, presenting great challenges to the world—this all sounds a bit exaggerated, Arian thought, rubbing his finger again.

"Bet you miss your cell phone more than anything," the Woman said, staring at Arian's finger.

More than anything? He stared coldly at the Woman.

Her eyes narrowed, meeting his, "Still get the cell phone ITCH, don't you?"

Again with the ITCH comment. The ITCH of cell phone addiction? Or my subconscious rubbing of my finger, my . . . ring? She wouldn't dare mention the ring, she wouldn't fucking dare! Blood pumped into his face. The Woman stared back and said nothing. Arian took a deep breath and dropped his shoulders.

"I do," he placated. She seemed to shrink away, receding slowly into the background.

"You seem to know a lot about current events, social trends, and . . . technology. Especially for not having any around," Arian looked around the room.

The Woman chuckled, a deep-bellied, self-satisfied titter, similar to the Pig's.

"You don't need to be addicted to social media or pumped full of mainstream news to know what's going on in the world," the Woman said.

"Quite the contrary," the Woman added. At this the Pig and the Woman attempted to hold back curling sneers.

All I ever saw here was an old radio . . . no cell phone or TV. Perhaps they read the papers and magazines, and I just never saw them. Maybe they hide them, only allowing me to see what they want me to see, Arian thought.

"Addiction is a real problem," the Woman said. "Food, drugs, alcohol, cigarettes. Not to mention pharmaceuticals and sex . . . addictions, yes. What else?" the Woman solicited like a teacher. At that moment Arian imagined her brainstorming on a white board.

"Gambling," Arian said, feeling patronized.

"Gambling and money addiction, yes," she said, nodding.

"Power, control" Arian jabbed at his oppressors. The Woman and Pig's faces were painted with a mix of surprise and guilty pleasure.

Touché . . . ?

"Are these addictions merely escapes? Do they free a person, or imprison them?" The Woman settled into herself, imbuing a philosophical air.

"I'm sure as hell not addicted to being imprisoned in a basement, and I'm sure as hell not free!" Arian said.

"Interesting," the Woman said, as if she was glad he'd finally said something about it. "Perhaps you're actually MORE free now than you were before?" She appeared suddenly dignified, comfortable, and proud—wearing her large frame as if it were a sign of wealth and power.

"Oh, and how is that?" impatience showed on Arian's face.

"Well, let's define 'freedom,'" The Woman said, poised.

King Pig was poised too, in his seat at her bedside, ready to be put to canvas by the brushstroke of a commissioned artistic genius.

The Woman went on: "'Freedom:' the ability, the free will, let's say, to act, speak, and think as one chooses."

"Oh, I must have misunderstood something. I thought 'freedom' meant the state of NOT being imprisoned or enslaved," Arian's sarcasm bit cleanly. "You talk about 'freedom' while I've been chained in your damn basement for weeks?"

"Is a basement any more of a prison than the trappings of our modern society? How many people working slave-wage jobs can honestly say that they are free? And the small percentage that do live in upper class society, are they free? Do all our possessions, conveniences, entertainments and technologies actually free us?"

"I imagine most people would prefer that as opposed to being locked in a basement against their will," Arian said.

"Interesting," the Woman said.

"Insane," Arian said.

"Stone walls do not a prison make, nor iron bars a cage," the Woman said.

"I beg to differ," Arian said.

"So you actually miss the constant social media distractions, viral videos, tweets and blogs constantly competing for your attention? Or should I say, 'depleting your attention?'"

Here we go again.

"You would trade the daily barrage of pointless mind-waste for silence? For some good old fashioned alone time? Free to get in touch with your deeper, inner self? An opportunity to reflect, meditate even? To be penitent?"

"You do realize, 'penitent' is the root word for 'penitentiary?'" Arian quipped.

The Woman grinned widely. She went on: "Perhaps you miss city life, with its smog, traffic jams, and endless concrete jungle—as opposed to miles of unspoiled desert, mountains, flora and fauna, where you are free to think, breathe, be? When was the last time you heard the buzz of a bee, the lament of a Mockingbird or a wolf howling in the distance? How about the hum of a Hummingbird? Or do you prefer the hum of your refrigerator? Oh such modern conveniences, yes. Where would we be without them? Oh, let's not forget about fast food! Of course you prefer a McDonald's Big Mac as opposed to fresh cut ham, or dare I say it, a chicken butchered by your very own hands?"

The Woman took a breath. Arian could sense where this was going and sensed too, that regardless of his response, nothing would change. He could argue his point only to be flooded with more counter arguments for the next hour, or he could more or less agree and get the charade over with. Arguing wouldn't change the terms of his imprisonment, but intensify them.

You cannot reason with madness, he thought. She held her eyes over him, two black beads prompting a response.

"More or less," Arian said finally, shrugging. The fight left him, and it seemed to increase her power.

"Less is more," the Woman's play on his words snapped back like a tennis return. Arian felt his energy wane, allowing the trickster to steal back the audience—her sleight of hands changed hands. She paused, watching as a quiet defeat hung over him.

"Another vital lesson for your generation," she said, salting the wound. "Or should I say, 'VIRAL' lesson?" She and the Pig laughed, wallowing in the double entendre.

"Fair enough," Arian said. Although it was a ruse, Arian began to feel a rare sense of 'freedom' in the ability to converse or debate. He'd long forgotten what a conversation or debate was like, other than imaginary ones in his head. Although he'd only said a few words and knew that it was likely all a ploy—as if his opinion had value—it did feel good . . . somewhat. Good as in normal. It was something to mitigate the onslaught of madness, a sprinkle of kindness on the dish of death, like a prisoner's last meal before being sentenced to the electric chair, or petting and hand-feeding livestock, before killing it.

"Learning lessons is what it's all about," the Woman said cryptically. She swung her eyes over to the Pig, who turned his head to meet hers.

"Isn't it, Gipp?" she said.

They laughed, letting it all hang out. There was no holding back. Their laughter sucked the energy out of the room like a collapsed star.

The mother's dead hearth, the womb of evil. Arian felt its tug. His body stiffened against it and he turned his head away. Their laughter beat into his skull, pounding away, as if his skull were a door made of thin paper.

Finally, he turned and said "Is that what you do, kidnap people, enslave and indoctrinate them?"

"Well, good help is hard to find these days," The Pig said, erupting back into laughter along with the Woman.

"And good pupils," the Woman chimed in, fueling their laughing fit.

"But why kidnap me, why risk getting the virus?" Arian said.

They stopped laughing, wiped tears from their eyes and swiped their drooling mouths. They composed themselves and stared blankly for a moment. The Woman spoke finally: "You don't think we're really concerned about the virus, do you?"

Arian's face drew tight with confusion.

"The Lord will protect us," the Woman said. The room fell silent.

"The Lord will protect you? Are you crazy?"

"THE LORD WILL PROTECT US," the Woman nodded. Arian's eyes darted back and forth between the Woman and the Pig's deadpan faces.

"Or he won't," Arian said.

They erupted into another laughing fit—reeling back, holding their jiggling guts as if dams were about to burst, their eyes tearing.

You can't reason with madness, Arian thought, watching as their laughter peeled back layers, revealing disturbing depths of narcissistic pathology.

"So what's your name anyway?" Arian asked after some time, knifing his way into their bubble. Their bellies continued to rumble in their laughter and they swooned back and forth, as if they didn't hear the question. Arian sat back and exhaled. Finally they settled into themselves.

"I said, 'what's your name?'" Arian repeated.

"Oh!" She turned to face him, "My name is Peggy," she said, bubbly as a schoolgirl. He imagined her much younger and innocent as she said this, in a cartoonish kind of way.

Auggie jumped into Arian's head. *C'mon, stay civil, keep things friendly.*

"I'm Arian," Arian said as the memory of their cryptic laughter rooted in his psyche.

"Oh, I know," she said.

"Huh?"

"I know just about all I need to know about you."

Arian's gut balled up like a fist, his skin crawled and the hair on the back of his neck stood up. They stared back at him with a shared clinical gaze, anticipating his next move. Arian swallowed hard then said, "Oh, yeah?"

"Yeah," she said.

"And Gipp here," Arian motioned with his head; "I take it, he is your husband?" Arian said in a game of quid-pro-quo.

"Oh, no," Peggy and the Pig again burst into laughter, but this time much stronger than before. Their bodies jiggled and the bed bounced beneath Peggy's weight. For a moment she seemed cured of whatever it was that sickened her. The same pull of gravity once again seemed to tug at everything around them. Arian drew into himself, shielding from its pull. Peggy and the Pig settled finally. She turned to him and said:

"Oh no, no, no. Ol' Gipp here, he isn't my husband at all," her words grabbed his attention.

"Don't be silly," she added.

"Well?" Arian asked.

"He's my brother."

Arian nodded, relieved the laughing fit had come to an end. It made sense that 'Peggy' and the 'Pig' could be brother and sister, given their age and resemblance.

"And so Tileper must be your younger brother?" Arian said. There was a brief, unnerving stretch of silence. She looked deeply into Arian's eyes, and with a probing perversity, said "Why, no."

Arian sat motionless, puzzled. Peggy's perverse stare probed deeper, and she said: "Tileper is our son."

❧

Kirsten dropped to the floor in a push-up position, then burst up to her feet, jumping straight up, hands above her head.

"Eight! . . . nine! . . . ten!" she said, pushing through the set of burpees. Following the female trainer on her TV screen, she then stood and threw a series of punch combinations.

"That's it, left, right, hook," the on-screen trainer said. Every muscle in her body seemed to burn, and the sweatband around her head, sports bra, and pants were soaked with sweat.

"Left, right, hook!" The trainer called out as Kirsten punched in sync with the pumping bass.

"Last set, let's go!"

Kirsten's triceps groaned in their extension, punching at life's demons—expelling the long work days at the hospital, worries of Arian, worries of a collapsing world.

The intensity of her beating heart and the amount of sweat bursting from her pores was her measure of how hard she worked, how numb she could get, how much she could distract herself. It was this boundary that she pushed each time. The closer she felt to complete physical exhaustion, the closer she felt to escaping the inescapable.

"Now back to burpees, c'mon!" The on-screen trainer cried out, dropping down to the push-up position. Kirsten followed. Her eardrums resounded with the sound of her deep gasps. Her arms burned, her legs shook. She pushed on, envisioning Arian safe and sound, back home in a virus-free world—living out their lives together, happy and, for a split-second, she had a vision of a newborn baby, cradled in her arms. *Happy thoughts*, she told herself.

"Five!" the trainer commanded. Kirsten sprang up from the floor, sweat dripping onto the yoga mat beneath her. At this physical and mental boundary, she felt the Warrioress within—fearless and ready to tackle anything life had in store for her.

"Six!" She repeated after the trainer. Her body struggled but the spirit of the Warrioress pushed on. She dropped down, did a push up, then sprang up to her feet again.

"Seven!" She held an image in her mind of her engagement ring. She divined its promise, and the growing symbolism it held— faith in overcoming insurmountable odds.

"Eight! Last two, let's get it!" Kirsten's arms became limp, pushing up from the floor, her legs shook beneath her as she sprung up, her feet barely leaving the floor.

The image of the ring transitioned back to a vision of her and Arian's first year together, Arian was holding her closely in his arms— two delicate bulbs in early flower . . .

"Nine!" the trainer called out. Kirsten exploded up from the floor, arms above her head, her body a fount of hot, boiling sweat. She dropped back down, "Ahhhhh!" She screamed, pushing up from the floor, her arms shaking, her legs heavy and slow to get beneath her.

"Ten!" In a final burst, Kirsten drew the last of her energy, the last vibrating molecule, the last particle willing to fight—the very last of her vital breaths. As she leapt, she felt a rush of air lift her up from the floor.

"Good job!" the trainer's voice rang out, applauding as Kirsten collapsed down and lay on her back. She splayed her arms out to her sides as if crucified. She fell into a dream state. Her consciousness disconnected from her body and she began to float away. She became a wispy, weightless being, a spirit of limitless light, off to a place where anything was possible. She wandered the astral plane, exploring great distances, buoyed by eternal peace. She could make out a bright pure light in the distance. As she approached it, it took on the energetic signature of Arian. They closed in with a central gravity, and together circled inward like spiral arms of a galaxy. Each trip around brought them closer to the center. Their energy became one, swallowed by an eternal calm—a complete oneness of pure light. And in the oneness, the Warrioress no longer was, for the battle for life had been won.

❧

Inbred, Luddite, mentally deranged, Arian thought, down on his knees, arms hanging from the chains in the light-stripped silence. *Haven't we seen enough inbreeding throughout history to know better? Cleopatra was said to have married both her brothers, right? The Roman emperor Nero's family tree didn't fork for generations back. I mean, you'd think the royals would learn after spitting out the likes of 'ol 'Bewitched' Charles ll, with his oversized tongue and hanging jaw . . .*

Arian recalled his college history notes; *They say he could barely eat his meals, or talk with that big tongue of his . . . that's it, ol' Tileper the Reptile is like a modern-day Charles ll—his hanging jaw, his close-set and crossed-eyes, those scaly, lizard-like fingers . . .*

Arian shook his head, *For Christ's sake.*

He rose from his knees and stood on stiff, shaky legs. Blood rushed to his head; he became lightheaded and nearly fainted. But as white specks flashed and the tingling sensation faded, he found himself standing upright, safe and conscious. Within the initial seconds of regained consciousness he found joy in the momentary escape. The world was new and for the briefest of moments he tasted freedom. It was like he'd arrived after a long, profound journey or a psychedelic experience. But just as the sensation came on in a liberating, out of body sort of way, it disappeared just as quickly, leaving him rooted in the physical once again, the here, the now . . . the solitude. Trapped.

The darkness took on a new meaning, a babe fresh from the bloody womb, released to a world of deeper stains—blood rivers flowing from the hand of bloody deeds. In the immediacy of a return to full consciousness came the morose and far too palpable . . . darkness. He was back in limbo, hanging . . . hanging from the chains.

The head rush was gone and left him washed ashore without a lasting sense of saltwater on his toes. The sun was dead and dried out, the sand as cold as ice. He was back, conjoined with his inseparable twin. He drew in a deep breath, filled his lungs then expelled it along with his ability to feel. He went numb, hanging limply in the silence.

Suddenly, there came a quick, flicking sound. His ears stiffened. Then the sound of a second flick, not far in front of him—below the ceiling. A moment later came the sound of a plate clinking down on the basement floor.

The Reptile? He must have come in while I passed out. But how long has he been here, standing over me, watching in the darkness? I didn't hear the hatch or his slither . . . I must have been out for longer than I thought.

The Reptile reached over and removed the duct tape from Arian's mouth and lifted his blindfold. The Reptile's vapory energy, his hanging jaw, dumb, underdeveloped boyish expression, and those lizard-like fingers took on a new dimension of morbidity. Arian's stomach locked up. He nearly gagged thinking about the fact that Reptile was inbred, and how much ugly sense it all made. The Reptile then unbound Arian's wrists. Arian's arms collapsed to his sides, sending crippling jolts of pain.

"Eat," the Reptile commanded.

"I'm not hungry," Arian said, diverting his eyes, which stung against the hatch-light, filtering down through the darkness.

"Water," Arian said, gagging. The Reptile stood over him, unmoving. There was an intense, discriminate look in his eyes.

"Please. I don't feel well," Arian said. The Reptile extended the bowl of water. Arian lifted his aching arm and took the bowl. As Arian drank, the water spilled down the sides of his mouth. Then came another flick of the Reptile's forked tongue. Arian curled forward over his knees and vomited at the Reptile's feet, toppling the water bowl, creating a stream of watery puke. Puke spilled down onto his shirt, lap and knees. Arian spent the next few minutes curled up in the darkness, heaving. Nothing else came up, but the pit of his gut burned with a dying gas, tearing away at his insides.

Suddenly, the Reptile snatched Arian by the arm and pulled him up. "Ahhh" Arian screamed as pain shot up his arm. "Quiet!" The Reptile pulled him up the ladder. He led him down the hall and past the kitchen. They exited out the front door, rushed to the back of the farmhouse, the sun stinging Arian's half-open eyes.

"Wait here!" the Reptile said, leaving Arian standing on shaky legs. He heard the squeal of a faucet, and looked up to see the Reptile dragging over a garden hose.

Hawk stumbled over the pebbly, dust-strewn plane and fell to his knees. He looked up as the black silhouette escaped towards the horizon, leaving eerie footfalls echoing behind. Hawk found his footing, rose and continued after him. The sky was a fireball swallowing everything up as if it was fuel. Devouring all, it spoke a cryptic tongue: 'the time has come.' Hawk shrank in fear as the fireball engulfed the air around him. He reached a hand forward as his legs propelled him—bending the last of his will towards the silhouette.

It glanced back over its shoulder—a mockingly formless face, forever fleeting. The skies burned, closing in on all sides and condensing matter down into a collapsing vortex. Hawk felt its pull—pulling as his outstretched hand grew nearer to the silhouette. The silhouette began shedding an inky blackness, burning past Hawk's face and was swallowed by the blazing sky behind him.

Hawk willed himself on, his legs drained of power, as a sharp pain knifed at his heart. The crimson sky and the silhouette's inky blackness continued to burn past Hawk's face and body, tearing at his hair and clothes. Hawk ran with all his strength and leapt. Extending both arms, he threw himself forward in a flying superman tackle. He screamed, emptying his lungs in a bestial catharsis. He tackled the silhouette to the ground. The silhouette scrambled beneath him, trying to hide its 'face.'

Hawk pinned its shoulders to the ground and reached towards its 'face,' tearing it away like a mask—revealing the pale, boney face of his father, which appeared like a dead sea captain. *I never wanted you!*

Father? Hawk said.

Leave me! Leave me! He cried in a Scottish-American accent. His red hair and beard suddenly burst into flames as he spoke, burning his pale, bony face. Hawk felt drawn to its danger like an adolescent experimenting with fire.

Father! Hawk reached for the face—to feel it, to know it as real. But as soon as his fingers got close, his father's face reverted back to a black, nondescript 'mask' once again.

Father! Hawk stripped it away—but his father's face was gone. A grave sense of futility rose up and Hawk screamed, *Noooo!*

Hawk threw the mask back over his shoulder, and it was swallowed by the approaching blaze. Immediately another blank mask appeared in its place.

Huh? Hawk tore it away, this time revealing the face of Arian. Arian's eyes were alight with idealism, and in them Hawk saw a decent, hardworking man. Their eyes became fixed as one, like binary planets, trapped in orbit. In them, helplessness expanded.

Help, please! Arian screamed. His eyes became disformed and discolored, pulling Hawk deep into their mysterious void.

Help me! Arian cried out, as his eyes morphed into the shape of a ring. Hawk lost himself in the ring's brilliance, and he felt as if he were drifting to some far-off place. It was as if the ring held the key to some ancient, unlocked mystery. Arian's ring-shaped eyes began to diminish in size, sucking Hawk further in, fading back into his face. The sky spiraled down like a churning furnace, and Arian's face disappeared back into a formless silhouette. It began to shed and was torn away and swallowed up by the blaze.

Noooo!! Hawk screamed, pulling at Arian's increasingly formless face. Again he tore away, revealing another blank mask. He tore and tore, each time more desperately, as mask after mask replaced the one before.

NO! NOO!! Hawk screamed. This time it revealed Kirsten's face.

Kirsten?! In her eyes too, he saw the ring. He stood staring into the rings as sharp pains jabbed into his gut.

The intense heat of the skies closed in on him. Surges of fear, guilt, and immense physical pain came over him. He tore at Kirsten's face and, just as he stripped her face away, it transformed into another mask. Thrown back over his shoulder, the mask burnt up with a flash, just as her dying voice cried out: *Find him!*

Kirsten!!! Hawk screamed, viciously tearing at the masks. They reverted back to a series of formless black silhouettes. He tore and tore at them, tossing one after another back over his shoulder. The silhouette continued to shrink from beneath him and the masks continued to regenerate. The body of the silhouette shrank down to the size of a child, then to the size of a doll.

Nooooooo!!! He screamed. He tore at one final mask. Once stripped, it revealed the face of a hawk. It had empty black eyes and a large scissors-like beak. It struggled beneath Hawk's weight, opening its beak with a harsh, grating cry: *Find him!*

Noooo! Hawk screamed, as the bird snapped at Hawk's fingers. Hawk felt the fireball-like sky tearing at his flesh, closing in all around him.

Find Him! the bird screamed one final time, just as everything was consumed by fire.

Hawk woke with a violent jerk, blinking away the image of the beak snapping in a vicious, choking death as the fireball claimed all. He found himself in the seat of his car, in the desert across the Interstate. His heart was thumping in his chest, his body heavy as a log, and he was bathed in a thin sheen of sweat. The intense transition to consciousness was both disturbing and cathartic. He felt like he'd completed a ritual of black magic, a rite of passage into darkness.

"Jesus Christ," he said, fogging the windshield with his breath. He rolled the window down and looked deep into the night. The sound of his breathing cut through the silence that lay over the land like a courtroom. The sky revealed a thin sliver of moon—an ominous waxing crescent hanging in the night sky. He reached up and thumbed one of the bear claw's on his necklace as the words repeated in his mind: *'Find Him!'*

❧

What do you think you're doing? Auggie said.

What? Arian hung from the chains in the basement.

Don't play dumb with me.

I'm not playing dumb.

What are you doing with that knife?

What knife?

Cut the crap, Arian! The damn knife in your boot.

Ah, you mean this knife? Arian dropped his eyes towards his feet.

Where'd you get it?

I snuck it from the kitchen.

Oh, just thought you'd arm yourself without them noticing?

There was a butcher knife, but it was too big and would probably be seen. So I figured a steak knife would do. A rare deviousness colored Arian's words.

Congratulations, you snuck a knife.

Slipped it under my belt while doing dishes, nothing to it. They didn't pat me down, Arian said.

No, but you know that they are watching you. I wouldn't be surprised if they know you have it.

Maybe. But why didn't they stop me then?

Another mind fuck. A ploy to let you think you are in control. You really think anything gets past the Pig? Besides, they've got guns, Auggie sounded like a parent.

Arian's eyes narrowed and his lips drew tight. A long, lulling pause drew out between them.

Or maybe they didn't happen to see you take it, but what if they discover it's missing, realize you're a threat, and kill you?

At least it will all be over with, Arian said, fatefully.

Don't give me that shit!

So what, you're gonna stab him at meal time, is that it? Auggie offered.

When he brings food to the basement, or when I use the bathroom, Arian said.

And what about the Pig? You gonna bring a knife to a gunfight?

Guess that's a risk I'll have to take, Arian said.

Well, you've clearly planned this out well, Auggie said, rolling his eyes. *You'd make a hell of an accomplice in a murder plot.*

Whatever, Arian shrugged his shoulders.

Whatever happened to waiting for someone to find the ring?

Their conversation took another pause and a palpable silence filled the air. It was a maddening silence that only the lonely, isolated know—a kind of comforting nothingness, free of the quotidian confines of routine, work or responsibility. But it was free of idealism, promise and goodwill too. It was free from hate, fears, and evils . . . emptied of everything, one had nothing to expect, nothing to gain. An

in-between place . . . a limbo of sorts. Nothing given, nothing taken . .
. just an empty, dreamless mindscape.

Finally, Arian began to speak, a half opening of his mouth
against the duct tape, eyebrows raised—but the words did not come.
His own mind wasn't convinced enough to form them. His thoughts
hung suspended in non-form and his chest filled with a sense of
wounded pride. Faith slipped away like a wisp of air through a crack in
a window.

*Arian, look. You've been kidnapped, demeaned and treated like a
slave. You're hungry, beat, and worried shitless. It's absolutely crazy, I
know. You're having imaginary conversations in your head, for Christ's
sake!* Auggie threw up two open palms. *I get it, I really do,* Auggie
assured.

Arian took a deep inhale with his nose, slowly letting it out, his
entire body deflating along with it. The silence resumed its dreadful
pace and Arian fell to its subordination.

But you're NOT giving up, Auggie said, finally. *That's a
Goddamn order, ya hear me?*

Arian hung motionless from the chains.

Ya hear me?

Yeah, Arian said with no show of confidence.

*If you're gonna plan an attack, we've gotta do this the right way,
ok?*

The right way?

Yes.

Whatever.

OKAY? Auggie commanded.

Yeah, okay, whatever, Arian's eyes flared against the dark world.

Just then, the hatch opened. Auggie backed into a dark crevice
in the wall, spying on, as the Reptile made his way down the ladder.
He slithered over to Arian and undid his wrists and took him up. The
Reptile led him through the house, out the front door, and left him
standing, blindfolded with just the sound of the Reptile's idling truck.

The smell of rotten eggs came from the tailpipe, mixing with the smell of sand baking in the sun. Arian stiffened, expecting a blow, but instead heard the sound of the tailgate lowering. The Reptile grabbed him and lifted him onto the tailgate.

"Lie down," the Reptile said. Arian lay on his side. The Reptile bound his wrists and ankles. Arian's heart contracted as the Reptile's scaly, lizard-like fingers nearly discovered the knife tucked into his boot as he tightened the rope around his ankles.

"Don't move," the Reptile ordered, slamming the tailgate to a close. Arian heard the camper shell shut, the driver-side door slam and, in a moment, he felt the wheels of the truck begin to crawl.

Peggy's voice came to him; *Freedom*, as once again, Arian exchanged one prison for another.

Meanwhile, Hawk sat in his car, in its usual place in the desert across from the gate and old ranch road; where he'd spent countless hours hunkered down in wait, a place now claimed as territory, earned little by little, over time. Time and patience were an investment with the promise of a return. His heels were dug in like an animal which evolved to survive and now reigned over the land—an apex predator with no subordinates to challenge the throne. Anything entering his domain was at his mercy. And he'd been running short of mercy as of late.

Hawk heard the distant hum of a motor and, looking in its direction, a growing cloud of sand and dust rose to the sky, trailing the same white farm truck he'd seen days before. It pulled up to the gate and stopped. He watched as the tall, lanky man from before got out and opened the gate, drove through it, got out, locked it behind him and then drove on.

Hawk flipped the ignition key and the car awakened like a beast lying in wait. The call to the hunt beckoned and the desert spirit commanded. Hawk slowly pulled onto the interstate and followed discreetly behind. What began as intuition grew to become an iron-clad certainty at the base of his gut. The fingers of his left hand were wrapped around the steering wheel as if clenching a reward, a prize worthy of a lifetime of effort, and his right hand rested over the butt of a revolver, holstered on his hip. He wore no expression on his face. The resolve in his gut, and the task ahead, would allow for no early celebrations.

❧

"I need to use the bathroom," Arian said, sticking a shovel into a mound of sand. He was back at the ranch, sweating over a hole he'd spent the last hour digging, as he'd done the last time he was there. He was leaning on the butt of the shovel, catching his breath as the dry desert air and heat of midday burned overhead.

"Bathroom," Arian repeated, looking over his shoulder at the Reptile, who was sitting beneath the shade of a tree with a shotgun over his lap. The Reptile answered back with his black eyes and Arian watched as evil danced ritualistically in them. A cunning little dance, and oddly seductive, it beguiled the Reptile's signature slack-jaw. The Reptile started to stand just as Arian rushed over with the shovel in both hands, held high above his head.

Channeling an ancestral line from a time when man was mostly beast, Arian roared, plunging the shovel into the base of the Reptile's throat, driving it in like a spear. Blood gurgled up from his neck as Arian put the full weight of his body behind the shovel, driving it deeper. Arian let out another roar so that the entire desert would know him. The Reptile let out a horrendous inhuman scream. The shotgun fell from his lap and he reeled back, jerking and bucking, his chin to the sky. He hit his head against the tree behind him.

The shovel stuck from Reptile's neck like a large toothpick, and Arian watched him squirm and writhe in pain as blood gushed from the wound like a broken water pipe. Arian drew the steak knife from his boot and, in a final burst, ran over and jammed the blade into the Reptile's gut. The Reptile curled forward, wrapping his fingers around the hilt of the knife, trying to pull it free. Blood drenched his shirt in thick red pools.

Arian staggered back, his legs wobbly beneath him. He dropped to his knees, watching as the Reptile's dark vapory energy fought its last battle, twisting in a tornado of death as the Reptile tugged at the hilt of the blade. He fell forward and collapsed into a fetal position on the desert floor. Blood continued to gush from his wound and the dark vapory energy dissipated once and for all.

Only in death will the Reptile be free of his evil and ignorance. Free, Arian thought, staring at the child-like vacancy in the Reptile's still black eyes.

The Reptile's grip around Arian's arm broke the vision, and Arian was back in his body, being led away, to the outhouse.

Jesus . . . must be the sun, Arian thought, as light-headedness added to the surreal effect of the daydream. The Reptile led him across a paddock to a dingy wooden outhouse with a slanted door that hung on loose hinges. A crescent moon was carved above the door. The outhouse looked like something witches or other Halloween creatures would use—like something out of a Tim Burton film.

The Reptile released Arian's arm, and stood facing the door, the shotgun holstered over his shoulder. Arian entered and closed the door. He lifted the toilet cover, undid his pants and sat. It was his second trip to the bathroom that day. What he really needed was a break.

The sun-warped, wood-panel walls fought back the heat, but trapped the horrid smell of feces inside. In the semi-darkness, he heard the buzzing of flies. He pulled his shirt collar up over his nose. Sweat rose like a vapor from his skin. In a few minutes the stinky, dingy shack was like a sauna. These tortures were nothing compared to digging holes beneath the naked sun, he told himself. His arms and back thanked him for the rest. His chest sunk inward as he embraced the sweat, the smell and the flies. He closed his eyes and disappeared.

He could find that place of non-being anywhere: that neutral place of non-feeling, non-existence, a nirvana-like place of eternal indifference. He could chisel that place out of the smallest stone, crawl inside and hide away in a pocket of warmth, a calloused skin of protection, a cocoon-like sanctuary. And for a brief time, if he cleared his mind and concentrated hard enough, he could actually find peace. No thought, no feeling, no identity, nothing but the void. Whether it was the dark basement, the hot tin-can of the truck camper or the smelly outhouse, he now knew how to find the ego-less self in nothingness. He drifted further and further away. Sweat steamed up the narrow-walled shithouse and flies stuck to his forehead. He was like a Buddhist monk, his mind separate from the external. No-thing-ness. Void. Peace.

"Hurry!" The Reptile commanded with a thunderous pull of gravity—a torrential downpour flushing the void down and dispersing it into the smallest cracks and crevices.

"Hurry up!" The Reptile repeated, his voice closer than before.

"I'm coming," Arian said, back in the here and now. He stood and, while rising, skimmed the fingers of his right hand over the knife in his boot. An involuntary twitch, a half-impulse shot down his forefinger. The vision of the Reptile curled into the fetal position and bleeding-out again came to him. Arian pulled the knife from his boot and held it behind him, obscured by his thigh. The image flashed across his mind once again. Arian pushed the door open with his free hand and stepped out—looking down the barrel of the Reptile's shotgun.

"Drop tha' knife," The Reptile said.

～

As the evening wore on, Arian's tasks took on deeper dimensions of psychological torture. Like the last time at the ranch, he collected eggs, killed chickens and cut pig meat. This time, he went through the motions of beheading the chickens with a detached, mechanical hand—numbed to the chicken's squawking appeals for life, and their after-death, full-body twitchings. Indifference had settled in; the pen was wet with ink, dripping over the contract with death. Arian's tasks were compounded by the stinging embarrassment at having been caught with the knife. He'd hoped that in the least, he would have had his fight, and if death came, so be it. But he couldn't fight against the barrel of a gun.

Abandoning his attack plan wilted his confidence, buried his pride in the sand. When he happened to make eye contact with the Reptile, it was a glaring reminder of defeat, and every time he turned to look over his shoulder, the Reptile was hovering over him like a prison guard.

You really blew it man, you—

Shut up Auggie, Arian thought. There was nothing to discuss, no headway to be made. He had but two choices now: plan another attack or continue to wait it out and hope for a rescue. Either option was a gamble, either potentially fed into the hand of death. But the question remained. *Would their knowledge of my plan to attack exacerbate the situation? Would they go ahead and kill me now that they see I'm a threat? They're not stupid. Surely they know I would kill them if I had the chance*, Arian thought.

What's with this ranch, anyhow? Does the Pig actually own it? He'd mentioned his grandfather had owned land. Is it connected to the farmhouse where the Pig and Peggy live, by some unknown road? Did we come here from the main highway? Or are we simply raiding a nearby ranch that was left abandoned, its inhabitants wiped out by the virus?

"Hurry," the Reptile said, derailing Arian's train of thought. Arian rushed to help the Reptile carry a large freezer to the back of the truck. They set it on the lowered tailgate and pushed it deep inside. The camper hatch was open like the mouth of a demon, and the Reptile's dark energy seemed to dwell there.

"Hurry up!" the Reptile boomed. Arian hurried along, following him back down to a cellar. They squatted down, and each took an end of the last of the industrial-sized freezers set against the cellar wall. The freezer was longer than it was wide—like a casket. Arian grunted, slipping his palms beneath its edges. His arms shook as they hauled it out.

"C'mon," the Reptile said. Arian's grip shifted as he took a step, nearly dropping the freezer.

"C'mon!" the Reptile repeated. Arian took another step, but his arms gave out and he stumbled. The freezer slipped free, tilted over and crashed down. The lid jostled loose and slid off. Arian looked over as the toppled freezer lay over the sand like an emptied casket; ice and frozen human body parts were scattered over the desert floor like various cuts of meat.

A single frozen eyeball, stared back at him like a dead fish—opaque, devoid. Arian curled forward, holding his stomach in a writhing attack of vomit and dry heaves. The Reptile rushed over to upright the freezer, snatching up severed arms, hands, legs and internal organs, frantically throwing them back inside. The Reptile singlehandedly leveraged the freezer up against the tailgate, using it as a fulcrum to slide it deep inside the bed of the truck. He picked Arian up by the collar and stood him against the tailgate. Arian shook violently, holding his stomach and spewing at the mouth.

The Reptile slapped Arian across the face, sending spit flying from his mouth. Arian shook his head like a dog shaking water off its body. With a swoop of his arms, the Reptile picked Arian up and sat him on the back of the tailgate. He reached into his pocket and pulled out thick rope ends. He quickly bound Arian's wrists and ankles, stretched duct tape across his mouth and re-blindfolded him. He shoved him into the back of the truck, shut the tailgate and camper hatch, got into the truck, and drove off.

Hawk emerged from the desert, pulled onto the interstate and followed behind the Reptile's truck as it rolled past. Hawk fell back and kept his distance—a mere speck in the Reptile's rear view, floating imperceptibly at the edge of sight. Hawk's eyes were drawn to the truck's camper. It was engulfed in a dark vapory energy, a mysterious veil of secrecy flirting along the edges of perception. There seemed to be a faint point of white light emanating from within it.

After some time the truck slowed and turned off the interstate, stopping in front of the locked gate. Hawk passed discreetly by, watching as the tall man with the farm hat and large hands got out of the truck and opened the gate. Just as Hawk passed by the truck, his ear perked up at what he could have sworn was a muffled cry coming from inside the camper. Hawk drove on for a moment, his mind abducted, taken to a far-off place. He shook his head, flipped the car around and drove back the way he came. The gate was closed and the truck had disappeared up the old country road leaving a dust cloud in its wake. Hawk pulled off the interstate, drove across the sand and reclaimed his hiding place among the rock and shrub, nosing the black car into the desert like a beetle. He killed the engine and took his cell phone from the center console. After ringing several times, finally police chief Dalton answered from the other end of the phone:

"Hawk, what can I do for ya?"

"Chief, it's time," Hawk said.

"It's time?"

"Yes!"

"Now I told you, we can't afford to gamble. If we're gonna move on this, we—"

"We gotta move, now!"

"You better be absolutely sure about this," Dalton said.

"Dead sure, get your butt down here ASAP!" Hawk hung up. He eyed the dust cloud trailing the Reptile's truck, watching as it settled over the desert with a dark vapor.

Staring at the specks of dissipating dust and vapor, Hawk thought; *You've danced your last dance.*

Arian was tied to a wooden chair opposite of Peggy, the Pig and Reptile. His bound wrists rested over his lap. His ankles were also bound, and around his waist ran a thick rope that strapped him to the chair. Peggy was sitting up in her bed and the Pig sat on a chair to her right, the Reptile to her left. The three of them wore long white gowns that fell to their feet, something like the pope and his papacy would wear. They wore long necklaces with Christian crosses. They had removed their hats and did their best to appear dignified.

A table at the foot of Peggy's bed separated them from Arian. A white cloth covered the table, and white candles sat burning on each end. Four empty wine glasses, two on each side, flanked an ornate silver chalice. The chalice claimed the center of the table with an air of elegance and ancient power. It was filled with a red liquid. Human meat had been dished out on silver plates. Everything was so carefully done, every detail tediously tended to, ritualistically laid by an expert hand.

The room was dark except for the flickering light of the candles, which cast dancing shadows along the wall behind the headboard of Peggy's bed. Arian watched as the light played across their faces and gowns. Their eyes shown as sinister red orbs.

Night had fallen and Arian could see the sky through the parted curtains of the window. If he had to guess, it was the witch's hour, a time when the veil between worlds was thinnest. One should take care not to let the demons slip in, because play they would. There was no other explanation for what Arian was witnessing except for insanity—his, theirs, and the world's.

Death. Yes, death, Arian thought. *Death to an insane world. And if this is death, I can accept it. The final chapter begins, the final scene set. A climax of flesh and blood, light and dark, life and ultimately . . . death.*

The actors are in full costume and the curtain is ready to be drawn. Give me my fight, give me my taste of blood. And when the final curtain drops, let it fall over my weary head and, in my remembrance, lay a piece of silver. Bless these tired bones and calloused hands with a silent prayer.

"AT-AR-AFF-MOOTSI," the Pig chanted. The Pig and the Reptile rose from their seats in unison as if an invisible string had pulled them up. They stood with straight spines and slightly upturned noses as pretentiousness beamed from their faces.

"AT-AR-AFF-MOOTSI" he repeated, as they hovered like dignified phantoms. The long O sound of 'MOOTSI' drew out, presiding over the moving shadows at their backs.

"AT-AR-AFF-SOOT," the Pig said. Peggy now joined them in placing their right hands over the crosses hanging from their necks.

"AT-AR-AFF-SOOT!!" The Pig punctuated the last word, which hung in the air as an echo. They shut their eyes. Silence gripped the room.

Arian's eyes drew inward and retreated. An intense feeling of guilt and an uncanny sense of indictment seized him. Eyes fully opened now, he felt he should pay attention. Even with their eyes closed, he felt they were watching, possibly now more than ever.

Am I about to witness a satanic ritual? Or is this merely theater? Why am I here? Do I really need to be present? Is the stage set just for me? And if it involves killing me, can you just get it over with? But give me my fight . . . my fight, yes.

He knew that even if he managed to get out of the bindings, the Reptile could easily catch him. And if he did somehow escape, his legs wouldn't carry him far. The story was forever the same: escape to where? Escape only to find himself in the middle of the desert? Left to erode along with the finite granules of sand, to wither away, dry up beneath the sun and choke out his last breath?

As much as he welcomed death, he couldn't die like that. He wanted his fight, yes. But how? When? He had been beaten, starved, used, demeaned and psychologically tortured. Was his drive for revenge greater than his willingness to survive?

Revenge, he thought. He shut everything out: Kirsten, his parents, his close friends. If he thought of them, he would crack. He filed them away as unthinkable—like the thought of ever being rescued or returned to a normal life. It was best to not think about any of that now. Hope, but not think. If he was going to die, then revenge was his final plea, his death wish. Blood—his last meal.

"AT-AR-AFF-MOOTSI," the Pig said. The Reptile stepped over to the plates of human flesh. He slid along, smooth as ever, unrushed, and ostensibly reverent—his spine erect, his head bowed. The Reptile served first Peggy, the Pig, then himself.

Arian thought for a moment that a dish would come his way, but no. Was he the lone spectator of this spectacle? They bowed their heads in a moment of silence before taking a seat and forking at the meat. They sat with the plates over their laps, the candle flames casting blood red shadows over their white gowns.

"I'd offer you a bite, but this is sacred meat, I'm afraid," the Pig said with a sneer.

"I'm fine, thanks," Arian said, surprised at the Pig's words, which broke the ritualistic air and dropped the theater down to an unanticipated informality.

"Human meat isn't exactly my thing," Arian said, casting his eyes on the floor, as their forks stabbed at the cuts of flesh.

"In some cultures it was considered an honor, an act of respect to eat the dead," the Pig said didactically, assuming his lecturer's tone.

"Respect? An' honor?" Arian shook his head.

"Honor thy father and thy mother," the Pig said. He, Peggy, and the Reptile—chuckled. Bits of flesh and saliva fell from their mouths, dotting their white gowns. Arian winced and looked away.

I can't believe it. They are actually eating human flesh! The flesh of a loved one? The Pig and Peggy's own father? The puppet master digs into his tool box, revealing his most sinister tool . . . their self-absorbed chuckling is not unlike that of a group of mischievous teens, unable to contain their latest gag . . . Christ, Arian thought, *It really is human flesh, isn't it?* He glanced up, wincing as his stomach turned. *This is insane.*

"Honor thy father," the Pig repeated, chewing with particular gusto.

"Thy father?" Arian challenged.

"Well, what better way to . . . keep it in the family?" the Pig said, raising a piece of forked meat from his plate as if in a toast.

"You're eating the flesh of your goddamn father?"

The Pig sneered widely.

"You sick fucks!" Arian exploded against his bindings, jerking the chair forward.

"We're just happy to have a guest for this . . . special occasion," the Pig said.

"You should feel honored," the Pig said, watching with a smirk as Arian winced.

"Honored?" Arian said, shaking his head.

"It is quite the occasion" the Pig said, smacking his lips as he chewed.

"Let me go! You sick, disgusting, excuses for . . ." Arian curled forward and heaved. Nothing came up. His eyes watered, his face flushed, the veins on his forehead bulged and his stomach tightened like a vice. The sound of their forks stabbing at their plates, the sound of their chewing, especially the Pig's—savage, open-mouthed, and salivating at the lips. Along with the wicked dance of the candle's shadows, it all conspired to invade his mind like a tactical war maneuver. Arian dry heaved again, curling forward over his lap.

"I don't feel well . . . I . . ." Arian managed to say between heaves.

"You're fine. A weak stomach is all," the Pig said with a laugh.

Arian glanced up at the Pig, as the other two joined him in chuckling.

"Besides, you wouldn't want to miss the best part," the Pig said. He and the Reptile then set down their plates and stood. The Reptile, subservient like a perfect little choir boy, took Peggy's empty plate. She settled back, poised like a Queen, watching as the Reptile dutifully stacked the plates on the table. The Pig took slow, short steps over to the table as if each movement held some significance—no room for wasted effort, as if the blinking of an eye could disrupt some mysterious conjuring. Arian felt another wave of guilt and entitlement, as if the breathing of air itself was a privilege not to be taken for granted. The Pig filled the four wine glasses with the red liquid from the chalice. Distributing it evenly between the glasses, he emptied it. The Reptile stood waiting.

The Reptile wins the Oscar, Arian thought.

"AT-AR-AFF-MOOTSI," the Pig raised the empty chalice with a slow, steady hand. He opened his eyes gradually with the rising of the chalice, inviting the wicked dance of candle light into his irises.

"AT-AR-AFF-MOOTSI," the Pig repeated. Peggy and Reptile repeated the phrase after him.

'AT-AR-AFF-MOOTSI?' What the hell is that, some strange form of Latin? Or complete bullshit?

"AT-AR-AFF-MOOTSI!" The Pig's voice boomed, louder this time. Peggy and the Reptile repeated after him one last time, much louder and clearer than before. They closed their eyes.

Arian's blood ran cold at the sight of the chalice—the Pig raised it to the heavens like a military general standing victorious over thousands of dead bodies, in celebration of a conquered empire. The Pig then lowered it, setting it precisely back in its original position. Arian again noted his careful, deliberate movement. The Pig handed Peggy a glass first, then the Reptile. The Pig took a third glass and stepped over to Arian. Arian tensed his brow and shot a defensive glance at the Pig. The Pig stood over Arian as unnamable, deified perversions crowned his head in a dark halo. The Pig looked down his nose, extending the glass.

"Take it," he said. Arian took the glass in the palms of his wrist-bound hands. He tilted it forward and eyed the liquid. He brought it to his nose and smelled it. He looked up and locked eyes with the Pig who stood over him like an apostle of darkness. Arian held firm, eyes steady, ready to unsheathe his sword.

The Pig's face flashed red, a deified stain—forever marked, his fate bound to the dark order like an executioner to his trade of death dealing.

"Drink!" The Pig commanded.

Arian took a sip. He turned his head and spat—blotting the wood floor with blood. The bitter, metallic taste stuck to the edges of his tongue. The Pig's mouth twisted into a mischievous grin. He then turned and stepped back over to the table. The Pig took the final glass from the table and stood in his former position beside Peggy's bed.

"First and foremost, we honor the all-father, God. Lord of the Heavens," The Pig said. They raised their glasses to the sky, then sipped in unison.

"We then honor our very own father—one hell of a man," the Pig added as Peggy and Reptile followed in raising their glasses and taking another sip. The Pig lowered his glass, smacked his lips.

"With the blessing of the Lord who watches from the heavens above, and with the blessing of our own father, who watches from the Other Side, together we welcome our newest member of the FAMILY," the Pig said.

Arian watched as they all sipped blood with cult-like mysticism. He wanted none of the Magic Kool Aid, but couldn't shake the feeling that the madness had already spread, that madness was a force that could not be denied. Once it laid its claim, only then does one truly know its seductive power.

"We are NOT family, you sick bastard!" Arian cried. The three of them turned their attention to Arian and stared blankly. Suddenly they burst into laughter. Arian coiled back, entangled in the puppet master's web of pull strings, watching as their sick, self-absorbed laughter roared up from a shared fount of depravity.

"No, no of course not," the Pig said, gathering himself. "I wasn't referring to YOU," the Pig's face drew tight. The bags beneath his eyes held up his eyeballs like Atlas holding up the sky, as all things sinister swam in the depths of his black pebbly irises.

"WE are welcoming the next generation into OUR lives," the Pig declared.

"What?" Arian said.

"You see," the Pig cleared his throat. "Peggy is pregnant," the Pig swept an open palm towards her. Her face seemed to glow, and there was a star-speckled galaxy behind her head, illuminating her lion-like mane in pure white light.

"Pre-g-nant?" Arian managed.

The Pig's face flushed with a red tinge. Arian trembled and heaved, "Pregnant?!" He repeated.

The Pig straightened his spine, a red dash of pride coloring his face. Arian jerked forward, pulling hard against the bindings, tilting the chair forward. The back legs of the chair came off the floor, and he fell head first, bouncing his forehead off the hardwood.

❧

Arian woke sometime later, his head throbbing with pain. He was bound to the chair, tighter than before. Peering through the narrow slits of waking eyelids, he found himself staring down the barrel of a shotgun.

"Good evening," the Pig said, aiming the shotgun at Arian's face. Each time the shotgun became less of a threat and more of a symbol. It became a sick, depraved formality, a forced acknowledgment of one's subordination. It became a tool of control, a weapon to wave over him, one of many puppet strings tugging against his free will, one of many extant reminders of his enslavement, but not his will to die. He was willing to die, yes. But one would need more than a shotgun to blast the life out of him.

"Are you going to shoot a defenseless man?" Arian scoffed.

"Well, the evil genius has delivered his manifesto, revealing his master plan," the Pig smiled behind the gun.

"The ceremony is almost over, the cycle nearly complete. Besides, we've wrung-out just about every ounce of use we can get out of the 'ol protagonist, don't ya think?" The Pig dropped the shotgun slightly, revealing two smiling eyes.

"Me, the protagonist? I'm flattered. No, I'm HONORED," Arian said sarcastically.

"Honored?" the Pig said.

"Yes, HONORED. One of your choice words, I understand," Arian said.

"So, if you're gonna do this, just go ahead and get it over with, will ya?" Arian added.

"Well, I did say the cycle was ALMOST complete," the Pig raised the shotgun back into position. Arian shut his eyes and sat up, defiantly squaring his shoulders and raising his chin. He would get his fight, yes. His fight was his refusal to give into their sick world, to taste the flesh and blood of another man, to denounce humanity for the sake of some bizarre ritualistic tradition . . . of cannibalism and inbreeding?

His fight was a moral one—he drew his sword for humanity, one that would not fall to the knees of such twisted ideologies and acts of cowardice. Physically, they can take his body, but they can't touch his soul. For the meek shall inherit the earth.

In the darkness of his shut eyes, Arian heard a sudden bang, an angry, howling report, ripping violently from the womb, a nasty spur from life to death, a sound borne dead with desperate immediacy. An even play by the hand of the Devil and God.

Arian slammed back against the chair. His heart leaped up into his throat. He felt immense pain, more terrible than anything he'd ever felt before. Then, in an instant, the pain was gone, overtaken by a formless white light and an overwhelming sense of peace. In his mind's eye he saw his life flash by in a slideshow of memories, tender sentiments, and visceral emotion. The smell of Venice Beach came to him and he felt frothy waves spreading between his toes. Then came the warmth and security of his father's cradling arms as he stood over the edge of the boardwalk, facing the sea. He saw his mother's bright blue eyes, and felt her kind, nurturing spirit leap out from every cell of her body. He saw himself alongside his high school pals, escaping away on weekend camping trips and beachside parties. He saw his college buddies and their dorm room parties, and he saw Auggie. He saw Kirsten. Kirsten!

"Now c'mon," the Pig said, lowering the shotgun from his shoulder. The Pig's words cut into Arian's imaginary world, and his slideshow collapsed into a single point of light and vanished. Arian looked down at his chest and the absence of blood, the absence of a wound of any kind.

What the—? A hallucination?

"Have some respect, will you? We are classy folk. You didn't really think we would just load you full of lead like that, did you?" The Pig dropped the muzzle to the floor and took his seat next to Peggy's bed. He rested the shotgun across his lap, leaned back and interlaced his fingers. The flames of the candles cast their last shadows, dying back in an eerie dance that seemed to slowly snuff everything out along with them.

"I'm surprised at you, Arian. I really am," the Pig said, assuming his erudite tone again. The Reptile stood, intently.

"There are other ways to go about this," the Pig said, as the Reptile slid towards Arian.

"Go about what?" Arian said, still waking from another world.

The Reptile reached behind his back and produced a steak knife. He stopped two steps in front of Arian and threatened with it as if it were more than just a weapon—as if it were a tool of black magic.

"Does that look familiar?" The Pig said, signaling the knife. It was the steak knife Arian had hidden in his boot.

"It seems you planned on doing some very nasty things with it," the Pig said with a look of judiciousness on his face. Arian furrowed his brow.

"And to think, we fed you. We provided a peaceful environment. Silence. An opportunity to reflect, contemplate, to seek within. We took you outside into the fresh air and unspoiled desert. We kept you alive, when we could have easily killed you. We even gave you front-row seats to this lil' private party here. Tsk-tsk. And all along you planned to hurt us," the Pig shook his head.

"You're sick!" Arian said.

"Well, as I said, we are civilized folk. Honest, hard-working, God-fearing folk," the Pig cleared his throat. "God-fearing," he repeated, as his words let loose a menacing silence, like the slow release of gas.

"Well, I would be lying if I said we didn't have a reason for bringing you here," the Pig added with finality. Something tangible lay encrypted in those words and sent shivers down Arian's spine. The Reptile's grip tightened around the butt of the knife and his vapory energy descended over Arian. The look in the Reptile's close-set eyes was no longer that of an innocent choir boy. Arian felt the curtain drawing to a close. He coughed as the vapory energy began to strangle the air around him.

"You see, we need a blood sacrifice to complete the ritual. Blood in, blood out," the Pig said, narrowing his eyelids.

"Blood sacrifice?"

"That's right."

"Why not kill ol' Tileper here, and use his blood? I thought you like to keep it in the family? Isn't that why you killed your father, and are now . . . eating him?"

"No, no, no. Of course not. We are civilized folk. Our father died of natural causes. It was his time. He left this earth when the Lord chose him to," the Pig said.

"Oh, and now that he's dead, figured you eat him, is that it?" Arian said.

"I guess you could put it that way," the Pig said.

"You're insane!" Arian screamed.

"Tileper, take him out back and . . . BAPTIZE him, would you?" The Pig again signaled the knife in the Reptile's hand.

". . . Wouldn't want to stain the floor," the Pig said. A full-toothed grin spread over his face. It was the cruelest, most debased thing Arian had ever seen. He knew then, that death had finally come. The Reptile came forward, slithering soundlessly over the hardwood.

Arian closed his eyes and thought, *That is the sound of death, finally come to claim me. Take this body, do what you will. But you can't have my soul, you cowards!*

The sound of the Reptile's near-imperceptible slither neared like the soft tolling of a funeral bell.

Suddenly, the door burst open, slamming hard against the inside wall. Arian looked over as three figures rushed into the room.

"Police! Drop the weapon!" Officer Snapp commanded, taking position to the right of the door, aiming a pistol at the Reptile with a two-handed grip. A second officer took position to the left of the door, aiming a pistol at the Pig. The third figure, Hawk, stood in the doorway, his hand reaching for the butt of a revolver holstered across his shoulder.

The Reptile lunged forward and jammed the knife into Arian's gut. Arian let out a deafening scream, curling forward over the blade. Officer Snapp squeezed the trigger and caught the Reptile in the shoulder. The shot sent him reeling back, leaving the knife sticking out from Arian's bleeding gut. Snapp took a second shot, which caught the Reptile in the neck and dropped him. As he fell, he knocked over the table, sending the chalice and plates tumbling down to the floor in a loud crash. The candles fell onto Peggy's bed, wicks burning at her feet and casting a chaotic play of light along the walls and ceiling.

The Reptile lay writhing on the floor, clutching his gushing neck, and shrieking in a high register. The Pig snatched up the shotgun from his lap, rose to his feet, cocked the hammer back and took fire, blasting Officer Snapp in the chest, sending him flying back, an arc of blood spraying into the air. He fell dead against the hardwood, leaving an impressionist-like trail of blood splatter across the floor. The officer standing to the left of the door fired off a shot, grazing the Pig's jaw, which caused him to reel back, jerking the shotgun up and blasting a hole in the ceiling. The Pig fell back against his seat, cupping his free hand over his nearly-detached jaw. Peggy pulled a pistol out from under her mattress, aimed it at the officer firing at the Pig and nailed him with two shots. He bucked back and fell lifelessly to the floor. Hawk fired at Peggy, hitting her in the forehead, sending her back, slamming hard against the headboard of the bed. Blood shot out from the back of her head like a busted water pipe, splattering the headboard and wall behind her. But in an instant before death, Peggy squeezed off a final round. The bullet caught Hawk in the shoulder and dropped him to his knees.

The Pig rose back up like a wounded hog, snarling grotesquely as his bloody jaw hung from his face—thick droplets of blood blotching his robe like a trickling waterfall. He pulled the shotgun to his shoulder and raised the muzzle. Hawk squeezed off two rounds. The first grazed the Pig's left eye, exploding it like a grape, the second caught him dead between the eyes. He fell backward and lay splayed-out over his chair, bleeding out like a king upon a seized throne. Even in death, there was a strange regal air about him.

Hawk rose to his feet and rushed over to Arian, who was slumped over in the chair, moaning low as the knife stuck from his gut. Hawk holstered his revolver and with two hands, pulled back on the knife, yanking at the hilt. Arian jerked back and the blade pulled free, blood gushing out along with it. Just then, police chief Dalton and a medic came through the door. Dalton stepped firmly over the hardwood and came to a sudden stop, silencing a walkie-talkie.

"What in God's name—?" he said, standing over the bodies of the two fallen officers. He ran his eyes over the Pig and Peggy's bloody, corpulent bodies, vested in white robes splattered with blood, and the puddling spill of the Reptile's neck wound and his twisted, contorted body lying on the hardwood. The fallen candles flickered their last, and the shadows against the walls fell like a dying puppet show.

"A medic! He needs a Goddamn medic!" Hawk yelled, undoing Arian's binds.

(A Few Months Later)

"Millions will be joining WHO's special online conference this weekend to celebrate the nation's flattening of the curve. Although there is still much work to be done, and continued safety precautions are still mandatory at this time, this is a major milestone in the fight against the virus. According to experts, the worst may well be behind us. Several international companies have been working hard to produce a vaccine, which experts say could be ready in less than a month. With the vaccine in place and a continued decline in the number of cases, a three-phase de-escalation plan will be put into effect, easing the nationwide stay-at-home order and allowing for the gradual re-opening of the economy.

The online conference will be acknowledging the efforts of our nation's heroes: medical staff, healthcare workers, emergency personnel, police officers, delivery drivers, grocery store workers and the like," the voice on the radio announced.

Hawk cut the volume and peered out of the lowered driver side window of his parked car, taking in the vast sweep of desert. It lay quiet and intractable like a carpet stretched beneath the distant mountain chain. His cellphone rang. He picked it up from the center console and brought it to his ear.

"Kirsten, hi."

"Hey Hawk!"

"I heard the news. Congratulations on flattening the curve. I'm happy for you guys, I really am," Hawk said.

"Thanks, it seems like the battle is finally turning in our favor."

"It's time to take a breather, enjoy some time off. You deserve it," Hawk said.

"Me and Arian are enjoying our time together at home, that's for sure. We've had enough excitement for a while."

"Tell me about it. How's he holding up?"

"His wound is healing and his online therapy sessions are going well. He's still a bit shaken, as you can imagine," Kirsten said. A long pause followed.

"But we're getting through it. He's a tough cookie."

"You are too. Thanks for hanging in there, being a monkey on Dalton's back. You really helped get his ass in gear. We made a good team," Hawk said.

"Damn right. Thanks for everything, really."

"Happy to help," Hawk said.

"How's the shoulder?"

"It's alright. 'Bout as good as my leg. I've got an 'old-man' shoulder to match my 'old-man' hobble now," Hawk said.

"Haha. So what's next for you, 'old man'?"

"Well, I think this 'ol dog has sniffed-out his last trail . . ." His voice fell silent.

"Your last rodeo, eh?"

"That's one inbreeding and cannibalism case too many. Time to hang up the gloves," he said with eyes over the desert.

"So they really tested negative for the virus?" Kirsten said.

"The tests came back inconclusive."

"Inconclusive?"

"Yeah."

"Strange. I guess we still don't know much about the virus. Jumped from an animal, like a bat, to humans. Started in a wet market in China, apparently. That's what they say, anyway."

"Crazy, eh?" Kirsten said.

"Well, the whole thing certainly was exactly that, CRAZY," Hawk said.

"Jesus, yeah . . . so that's really it for you, eh? Off to retire on some tropical island somewhere?"

"Naw, tropical islands never were quite my thing," Hawk's eyes softened over the desertscape.

"I see."

"Think I'll stick around—stay rooted right here in the L.A. area," Hawk said. "I don't foresee any distant travels in my near-future. Instead of going looking for things, I think I'll let things come to me."

"Sounds about right."

"Besides, I think I've finally found what I've been looking for."

"Yeah? What's that?"

"The desire to stop looking."

"Well whatever you decide to do, you 'ol dog," Kirsten said after some reflection, "Don't forget to drop us a line from time to time."

"I'll be around," he said.

"Sounds good. Glad you're doing well," Kirsten said.

"You too. And thanks again for all that you guys n' gals do out there, on the front line. You're the real heroes," Hawk said.

"Thanks, really."

"Take care."

Hawk hung up and looked past the metal gate to the road that had led to the Pig's old farm house. His thoughts grew heavy with the memory of Arian, Kirsten and the hunt . . . *the hunt*, he thought. *Who needs to hunt anything? We're all going so fast; hunting, chasing, seeking . . . we run in place, spinning our wheels. What're we seeking? Where're we going? Do we ever really arrive? Is there such a thing?* He pulled his eyes from the old road, turned on the ignition and drove over the flat desert floor towards the interstate. *Slow it down and let it come.* As he pulled onto the interstate and headed towards the horizon, a black silhouette appeared suddenly in his rear view mirror. He continued on, undaunted. *Because come it will.* Eyes ahead, he left the desert behind one final time.

THE END

AUTHOR HARLAN WELLS

Harlan Wells was born in Portland, Oregon in 1982. At the age of seven, his family moved to California and settled in Mendocino County.

Decidedly athletic, it wasn't until 2004 that Harlan began to write. His love of travel took him across the United States, while documenting his experiences in travelogues.

While attending San Francisco Community College in 2011, it was during a creative writing course that confidence in his writing began to build. He won the grand prize of the One in A Million essay contest, as well as had an essay selected for publication for the College Inquirer that same year.

He has spent the last several years living, working and traveling through countries such as Taiwan, India, Indonesia, Australia, and New Zealand, writing memoirs and fiction along the way. He then backpacked much of Western Europe and has resided in Spain since 2017, continuing to draw inspiration for his writings.

In 2016, two works of fiction were self-published by the author: *Dream Revenge,* and *Footprint Flats.* In 2019, he published a fiction collection called *Goose and Other Short Stories.*